My Naughty Little Sister COLLECTION

DOROTHY EDWARDS

ILLUSTRATED BY
Shirley Hughes

Farshore

For my sister, Phil

Farshore

First published in Great Britain 1968
by Methuen Children's Books Ltd
This edition published 2017
by Farshore

An imprint of HarperCollins*Publishers*
1 London Bridge Street, London SE1 9GF

farshore.co.uk

HarperCollins*Publishers*
1st Floor, Watermarque Building,
Ringsend Road, Dublin 4, Ireland

Text copyright © 1952 The Estate of Dorothy Edwards
Illustrations copyright © 1952 Shirley Hughes
Cover illustration copyright © 2007 Shirley Hughes

The moral rights of the illustrator have been asserted

ISBN 978 1 4052 9402 7
Printed in Great Britain by CPI Group
3

Stay safe online. Any website addresses listed in this book are correct at the
time of going to print. However, Farshore is not responsible for content
hosted by third parties. Please be aware that online content can be subject
to change and websites can contain content that is unsuitable for children.
We advise that all children are supervised when using the internet.

MIX
Paper from
responsible sources
FSC™ C007454

This book is produced from independently certified FSC™ paper
to ensure responsible forest management.

For more information visit: www.harpercollins.co.uk/green

Contents

My Naughty Little Sister

Contents

Contents *continued*

1. Going fishing

A long time ago when I was a little girl, I had a sister who was littler than me. My little sister had brown eyes, and red hair, and a pinkish nose, and she was very, very stubborn.

When you told her to smile for her photograph, she said, 'No, I don't want to,' but if you gave her an ice-cream, or a chocolate biscuit, or a toffee-drop, she said 'Thank you,' and smiled and smiled.

So you must try to imagine her with a chocolate biscuit *and* an ice-cream *and* a toffee-drop, so that you can see her at her very, very best . . .

Imagine very hard . . . There, doesn't she look a bright, happy child?

Well now, I'm going to tell you some stories about her which I think you will like.

The very first story is called *Going Fishing* and here it is:

One day, when I was a little girl, and my sister was a very little girl, some children came to our house and asked my mother if I could go fishing with them.

They had jam-jars with string on them, and fishing-nets and sandwiches and lemonade.

My mother said, 'Yes' – I could go with them; and she found *me* a jam-jar and a fishing-net, and cut *me* some sandwiches.

Then my naughty little sister said, 'I want to go! I want to go!' Just like that. So my mother said I might as well take her too.

Then my mother cut some sandwiches for my little sister, but she didn't give her a jam-jar or a fishing-net because she said she was too little to go near the water. My mother gave my little sister a basket to put stones in, because my little sister liked to pick up stones, and she gave me a big bottle of lemonade to carry for both of us.

My mother said, 'You mustn't let your little sister get herself wet. You must keep her away from the water.' And I said, 'All right, Mother, I promise.'

So then we went off to the little river, and we took our shoes off

and our socks off, and tucked up our clothes, and we went into the water to catch fish with our fishing-nets, and we filled our jam-jars with water to put the fishes in when we caught them. And we said to my naughty little sister, 'You mustn't come, you'll get yourself wet.'

Well, we paddled and paddled and fished and fished, but we didn't catch any fish at all, not one little tiny one even. Then a boy said, 'Look, there is your little sister in the water too!'

And, do you know, my naughty little sister had walked right into the water with her shoes and socks on, and she was trying to fish with her little basket.

I said, 'Get out of the water,' and she said, 'No.'

I said, 'Get out at *once*,' and she said, 'I don't want to.'

I said, 'You'll get all wet,' and she said, 'I don't care.' Wasn't she naughty?

So I said, 'I must fetch you out then,' and my naughty little sister tried to run away in the water. Which is a silly thing to do because she fell down and got all wet.

She got her frock wet, and her petticoat wet, and her knickers wet, and her vest wet, and her hair wet, and her hair-ribbon – all soaking wet. Of course, I told you her shoes and socks were wet before.

And she cried and cried.

So we fetched her out of the water, and we said, 'Oh, dear, she will catch a cold,' and we took off her wet frock, and her wet petticoat and her wet knickers and her wet vest, and her wet hair-ribbon, *and* her wet shoes and socks, and we hung all the things to dry on the bushes in the sunshine, and we wrapped my naughty little sister up in a woolly cardigan.

My little sister *cried and cried*.

So we gave her the sandwiches, and she ate them all up. She ate up her sandwiches and my sandwiches, and the other children's sandwiches all up – and she cried and cried.

Then we gave her the lemonade and she spilled it all over the grass, and she cried and cried.

Then one of the children gave her an apple, and another of the children gave her some toffees, and while she was eating these, we took her clothes off the bushes and ran about with them in the sunshine until they were dry. When her clothes were quite dry, we put them all back on her again, and she screamed and screamed because she didn't want her clothes on any more.

So, I took her home, and my mother said, 'Oh, you've let your little sister fall into the water.'

And I said, 'How do you know? Because we dried all her clothes,' and my mother said, 'Ah, but you didn't *iron* them.' My little sister's clothes were all crumpled and messy.

Then my mother said I should not have any sugary biscuits for supper because I was disobedient. Only bread and butter, and she said my little sister must go straight to bed, and have some hot milk to drink.

And my mother said to my little sister, 'Don't you think you were a naughty little girl to go in the water?'

And my naughty little sister said, 'I won't do it any more, because it was too wet.'

But, do you know, when my mother went to throw away the stones out of my little sister's basket, she found a little fish in the bottom which my naughty little sister had caught!

2. My Naughty Little Sister at the fair

Here is another story about my naughty little sister.

When I was a little girl, my little sister used to eat all her breakfast up, and all her dinner up, and all her tea up, and all her supper up – every bit.

But one day my naughty little sister wouldn't eat her breakfast. She had cornflakes and an egg, and a piece of bread and butter, and an apple, and a big cup of milk, and she wouldn't eat anything.

She said, 'No cornflakes.'

Then my mother said, 'Well, eat your egg,' and she said, 'No egg. Nasty egg.' She said, 'Nasty apple,' too, and she spilled her milk all over the table. Wasn't she naughty?

My mother said, 'You won't go to the fair this afternoon if you don't eat it all up.' So then my naughty little sister began to eat up her breakfast very quickly. She ate the cornflakes and the egg, but she really couldn't manage the apple, and my mother said, 'Well, you ate most of your breakfast so I think we shall let you go to the fair.'

Shall I tell you why my naughty little sister hadn't wanted to eat her breakfast? *She was too excited.* And when my naughty little sister was excited, she was very cross and disobedient.

When the fair-time came, my big cousin Jane came to fetch us. Then my naughty little sister got so excited that she was crosser than ever. My mother dressed her up in her new best blue dress and her new best blue knickers, and her white shoes and blue socks, but my naughty little sister wouldn't help a bit. And you know what that means.

She went all stiff and stubborn, and she wouldn't put her arms in the armholes for herself, and she wouldn't lift up her feet for her shoes, and my mother said, 'Very well, they shall go without you.' Then my naughty little sister lifted up her feet very quickly. Wasn't she bad?

We went on a bus to the fair, and when we got there, it was very nice. We saw cows and horses and pigs and sheep and chickens, and lots and lots of people. And there were big swings that went swingy-swing, swingy-swing, and roundabouts that went round and round, round and round. Then my naughty little sister said, 'I want a swing! I want a swing!'

But my big cousin Jane said, 'No, you are too little for those big swings, but you shall go on the little roundabout.'

The little roundabout had wooden horses with real reins, and things to put your feet in, and there were little cars on the roundabout, and a little red fire-engine, and a little train.

First, we watched the roundabout going round and round, and when it

went round all the cars and horses went up and down, up and down, and the fire-engine and the train went up and down too. The roundabout played music as it went round.

Then, when it stopped, my big cousin said, 'Get on, both of you.' There were lots of other children there, and some of them were afraid to go on the roundabout, but my little sister wasn't afraid. She was the first to go on, and she got on all by herself, without *anyone* lifting her at all. Wasn't she a big girl? And do you know what she did? She got into the seat of the red fire-engine, and rang and rang the bell. 'Clonkle! Clonkle! Clonkle!' went the bell, and my little sister laughed and laughed, and when the roundabout went round it played nice music, and my naughty little sister said, 'Hurrah. I'm going to put the fire out!'

My little sister had four rides on the roundabout. One, two, three, four rides. And then my big cousin Jane said, 'We have spent all our money. We will go and look at the people buying horses.'

But my little sister got thoroughly nasty again, and she said, 'No horse. Nasty horses. Want roundabout.' There, wasn't that bad of her? I'm glad you're not like that.

But my cousin said, 'Come along at once,' and my naughty little sister had to come, but do you know what she did, while we were looking at the horses? *She ran away*. I said she was a naughty child, you know.

Yes. She ran away, and we couldn't

find her anywhere. We looked and looked. We went to the roundabouts and she wasn't there. We went to the swings and she wasn't there. She wasn't at the pig place, or the cow place or the chicken place, or any of the other places. So then my big cousin Jane said, 'We must ask a policeman. Because policemen are good to lost children.'

We asked a lady if she could tell us where a policeman was, and the lady said, 'Go over the road to the police-station.'

So my cousin took me over the road to the police-station, and we went into a big door, and through another door, and we saw a policeman sitting without his hat on. And the policeman said, 'How do you do, children. Can I help you?' Wasn't that nice of him?

Then my big cousin Jane said, 'We have lost a naughty little girl.' And she told the nice policeman all about my bad little sister, all about what her name was, and where we had lost her, and what she looked like, and the nice policeman wrote it all down in a big book.

Then the kind policeman said, 'No, we haven't a little girl here, but if we find her, we will send her home to you in a big car.'

So then my cousin Jane and I went home, and it was a long walk, because we had spent all our pennies on the roundabout.

When we got home, what do you think? There was my naughty little sister, sitting at the table, eating her tea. She had got home before us after all. And do you know why that was? It was because a kind policeman had found her and taken her home in his big car.

And do you know, my naughty little sister said she'd never, never run off like that again, because it wasn't at all nice, being lost. She said it made her cry.

But, my naughty
little sister said,
if she did
get lost
again, she
would find
another nice
policeman
to take her

home, because policemen are so kind
to lost children.

3. When My Naughty Little Sister wasn't well

I hope you aren't a shy child. My naughty little sister wasn't shy, but she used to pretend to be sometimes, and when nice aunts and uncles came to see us, she wouldn't say, 'How do you do!' or shake hands or anything, and if they tried to talk to her she would run off down the garden and hide among the currant bushes until they went away.

But my naughty little sister talked and talked when she wanted to. She talked to the milkman and the baker and the coalman and the window-cleaner man, and all the other people who came to the door, and when they came she got terribly in their way, because she talked to them so much, but they all liked my naughty little sister.

One day she upset all the milkman's bottles, and he only said, 'Never mind, no use crying over spilt milk,' and another day she shut the cellar up just as the coalman was going to tip the coal in, and he only said, 'Well, well now, there's a job for your father!' and she climbed up the ladder after the window-cleaning man and then she cried because she was afraid to come down, but *he* only said, 'There! There! Don't cry, dearie,' and he lent her his leathery thing to wipe her tears on.

So you see, they liked my naughty little sister very much, but wasn't she naughty?

Well now, one day my poor naughty little sister wasn't very well. She sat in her chair and looked very miserable and said, 'I'm not a very well girl today.'

So my mother said, 'You shall go to bed and have a hot drink, and a hot-water-bottle and we shall send for the doctor to come and see what's wrong with you.'

And my naughty little sister said, 'No doctor! Nasty doctor!' Wasn't she a silly cuckoo? Fancy saying, 'No doctor' when she wasn't well!

But my mother said, 'He's a nice doctor. You must tell him how you feel, and then he will make you all better.'

Then my naughty little sister said, 'I'm too shy. I *won't* talk to him.' She said it in a cross, growly voice, 'I won't talk to him!'

So my naughty little sister went to bed, and she had a hot-water-bottle and a hot drink. Also, she had her best books, and all her dolls and her teddy bears, but she felt so not-well that she didn't want any of these things at all.

Presently my naughty little sister heard a knock on the front door, and she said, 'No doctor,' and hid her face under the sheet.

But it wasn't the doctor, it was the nice milkman, and when he heard my naughty little sister wasn't well, he sent her his love, and a notebook with lines on, and a blue pencil to write with.

Then my naughty little sister heard the front door again, and she said, 'No doctor,' again, and hid her face again, but it was the nice baker, and he sent my naughty little sister *his* love and a little spongy cake in case she fancied it.

Then she heard the front door again, and she said, 'No doctor – nasty doctor,' but it was the nice coalman, and he sent my naughty little sister *his* love and a red rose from his cap that smelt rosy and coaly.

After that my naughty little sister began to feel a much happier girl, and she didn't hide her face any more, so that when the window-cleaner man came to clean the window, she could see him smiling through the glass, and when he popped his head in and asked, 'How's the invalid?' my naughty little sister said, 'I'm not a well girl today.'

The window-cleaner man said, 'Well, the doctor will soon put you right.'

And my naughty little sister watched the window-cleaner man rubbing away with the leathery thing, and then she said, 'No doctor,' to the

window-cleaner man. 'No doctor,' she said, out loud.

'Yes doctor,' said the window-cleaner man.

'No doctor,' said my naughty little sister.

'That's a silly idea you've got,' said the window-cleaner man. 'The doctor will make you a well girl again.'

Then my naughty little sister began to cry and cry. 'No doctor, no doctor. I'm too shy.' Like that, in that miserable way.

And then the window-cleaner man said, 'What a pity you won't have the doctor, because you won't see his listening-thing, or his glass-stick-thing to pop under your tongue, or the doctor's bag that he keeps his little bottles in.'

Then my naughty little sister stopped crying and said, 'What listening-thing? What stick-thing?'

'Ah,' said the window-cleaner man, 'I shan't tell you that. Why should I? But it's a pity you won't see that doctor and find out for yourself.' That's what the window-cleaner man said.

Then the window-cleaner man went away, and took his ladder with him, and my naughty little sister stayed in her bed and thought and thought.

And presently, when she heard a knock at the front door, my naughty little sister didn't say, 'No doctor,' and hide her face under the sheet, even though it really *was* the doctor this time. She didn't do anything silly like that at all.

My naughty little sister waited and waited until she heard my mother coming upstairs with the doctor, and when the doctor came into her bedroom my naughty little sister didn't say, 'Go away,' or pretend to be shy, or scream, or do any of the bad things she could do.

She said, 'Hallo, doctor,' and then the doctor said, 'Hallo, and how are you today?' and my naughty little sister said, 'I'm not a well girl today.'

Then she said, 'Have you got your doctor's bag, and your listening-thing, and your glass-stick-thing to pop into my mouth?' and the doctor said, 'Yes, I have.'

Then my naughty little sister was pleased as pleased, and she liked the doctor so much after all, that she took all the medicine he sent her without being cross once, and got a well girl again very quickly.

4. My Naughty Little Sister makes a bottle-tree

One day, when I was a little girl, and my naughty little sister was a littler girl, my naughty little sister got up very early one morning, and while my mother was cooking the breakfast, my naughty little sister went quietly, quietly out of the kitchen door, and quietly, quietly up the garden-path. Do you know why she went *quietly* like that? It was because she was *up to mischief*.

She didn't stop to look at the flowers, or the marrows or the runner-beans and she didn't put her fingers in the water-tub. No! She went right along to the tool-shed to find a trowel. You know what trowels are, of course, but my naughty little sister didn't. She called the trowel a 'digger'.

'Where is the digger?' said my naughty little sister to herself.

Well, she found the trowel, and she took it down the garden until she came to a very nice place in the big flower-bed. Then she stopped and began to dig and dig with the trowel, which you know was a most naughty thing to do, because of all the little baby seeds that are waiting to come up in flower-beds sometimes.

Shall I tell you why my naughty little sister dug that hole? All right. I will. It was because she wanted to plant a brown shiny acorn. So, when she had made a really nice deep hole, she put the acorn in it, and covered it

all up again with earth, until the brown shiny acorn was all gone.

Then my naughty little sister got a stone, and a leaf, and a stick, and she put them on top of the hole, so that she could remember where the acorn was, and then she went indoors to have her hands washed for breakfast. She didn't tell me, or my mother or anyone about the acorn. She kept it for her secret.

Well now, my naughty little sister kept going down the garden all that day, to look at the stone, the leaf and the stick, on top of her acorn-hole, and my naughty little sister smiled and smiled to herself because she knew that there was a brown shiny acorn under the earth.

But when my father came home, he was very cross. He said, 'Who's been digging in my flower-bed?'

And my little sister said, 'I have.'

Then my father said, 'You are a bad child. You've disturbed all the little baby seeds!'

And my naughty little sister said, 'I don't care about the little baby seeds, I want a home for my brown shiny acorn.'

So my father said, 'Well, *I* care about the little baby seeds myself, so I shall dig your acorn up for you, and you must find another home for it,' and he dug it up for her at once, and my naughty little sister tried all over the garden to find a new place for her acorn.

But there were beans and marrows and potatoes and lettuce and tomatoes and roses and spinach and radishes, and no room at all for the acorn, so my naughty little sister grew crosser and crosser and when tea-time came she wouldn't eat her tea. Aren't you glad you don't show off like that?

Then my mother said, 'Now don't be miserable. Eat up your tea and you shall help me to plant your acorn in a bottleful of water.'

So my naughty little sister ate her tea after all, and then my mother, who was a clever woman, filled a bottle with water, and showed my naughty little sister how to put the acorn in the top of the bottle. Shall I tell you how she did it, in case you want to try?

Well now, my naughty little sister put the pointy end of the acorn into the water, and left the bottom of the acorn sticking out of the top – (the bottom end, you know, is the end that sits in the little cup when it's on the tree).

'Now,' said my mother, 'you can

watch its little root grow in the water.'

My naughty little sister had to put her acorn in lots of bottles of water, because the bottles were always getting broken, as she put them in such funny places. She put them on the kitchen window-sill where the cat walked, and on the side of the bath, and inside the bookcase, until my mother said, 'We'll put it on top of the cupboard, and I will get it down for you to see every morning after breakfast.'

Then at last, the little root began to grow. It

pushed down, down into the bottle of water and it made lots of other little roots that looked just like whitey fingers, and my naughty little sister was pleased as pleased. Then, one day, a little shoot came out of the top of the acorn, and broke all the browny outside off, and on this little shoot were two tiny baby leaves, and the baby leaves grew and grew, and my mother said, 'That little shoot will be a big tree one day.'

My naughty little sister was very pleased. When she was pleased she danced and danced, so you can just guess how she danced to think of her acorn growing into a tree.

'Oh,' she said, 'when it's a tree we can put a swing on it, and I can swing indoors on my very own tree.'

But my mother said, 'Oh, no. I'm afraid it won't like being indoors very much now, it will want to grow out under the sky.'

Then my naughty little sister had a good idea. And now, this is a *good thing* about my little sister – she had a *very kind thought* about her little tree. She said, 'I know! When we go for a walk we'll take my bottle-tree and the digger' (which, of course, you call a trowel) 'and we will plant it in the park, just where there are no trees, so it can grow and grow and spread and spread into a big tree.'

And that is just what she did do. Carefully, carefully, she took her bottle-tree out of the bottle, and put it in her little basket, and then we all went out to the park. And when my little sister had found a good place for her little bottle-tree, she dug a nice deep hole for it, and then she put her tree into the hole, and gently, gently put the earth all round its roots, until only the leaves and the stem were showing, and when she'd planted it in, my mother showed her how to pat the earth with the trowel.

Then at last the little tree was in the kind of place it really liked, and my little sister had planted it all by herself.

Now you will be pleased to hear that the little bottle-tree grew and grew and now it's quite a big tree. Taller than my naughty little sister, and she's quite a big lady nowadays.

5. The wiggly tooth

When I was a little girl, and my naughty little sister was a very little girl, we used to have an apple tree in our garden, and sometimes my naughty little sister used to pick the apples and eat them. It was a very easy thing to do because the branches were so low.

So, my mother told us we were not to pick the apples. My mother said, 'It is naughty to pick the apples when they are growing upon the tree, because we want them to go on growing until they are ripe and rosy, and then we shall pick them and put them quite away for the winter-time.'

'If you want an apple,' my mother said, 'you must pick up a windfall and bring it to me, and I will wash it for you.'

As you know, 'windfalls' are apples that fall off the tree on to the grass, so, one day, my little sister looked under the tree and found a nice big windfall on the grass, and she took it in for my mother to wash.

When my mother had washed the apple, *and* cut out the specky bit where the little maggot had gone to live, my little sister sat down on the step to eat her big apple.

She opened her mouth very wide, because it *was* such a big apple, and she took a big bite. And what do you think happened? She felt a funny cracky sort of feeling in her mouth. My naughty little sister was so surprised that she nearly tumbled off the step when she felt the funny cracky feeling in her mouth, and she put in her finger to see what the crackiness was, and she found that one of her nice little teeth was loose.

So my naughty little sister ran indoors to my mother, and she said,

'Oh, dear, my tooth has gone all loose and wiggly, what shall I do?' in a waily whiny voice because at first she didn't like it very much.

My mother said, 'There's nothing to worry about. All your nice little baby-teeth will come out one by one to make room for your big grown-up teeth.'

'Have a look, have a look,' said my naughty little sister. So my mother had a look, and then she said, 'It's just as I thought, there is a new little tooth peeping through already.'

So after that my little sister had a loose tooth, and she used to wiggle it and wiggle it with her finger. She used to wiggle it so much that the tooth got looser and looser.

When the nice baker came, my naughty little sister showed him the tooth, and she showed the milkman and the window-cleaner man, and sometimes she used to climb up to the mirror and wiggle it hard, to show herself, because she thought that a loose tooth

was a very special thing to have.

After a while, my mother said, 'Your tooth is so very loose, you had better let me take it out for you.'

But my naughty little sister didn't want to lose her lovely tooth, because she liked wiggling it so much, and she wouldn't let my mother take it out at all.

Then my mother said, 'Well, pull it out yourself then,' and my silly little sister said, 'No, I like it like this.'

The next time the window-cleaner man came, he said, 'Isn't that toothy-peg out yet?'

And my naughty little sister said,

'No. It's still here.' And she opened her mouth very wide to show the window-cleaner man that it was still there.

The window-cleaner man said, 'Why don't you pull it out? It's hanging on a threddle, it is indeed.'

My naughty little sister told him that she liked to have it to wiggle and to show people.

So the window-cleaner man said, 'You'd better take it to show the dentist.'

My naughty little sister said why should she take it to the dentist? Because she hadn't heard much about dentists, and the window-cleaner man who knew all about doctors and dentists and about how the sun moves and how pumpkins grow, told my naughty little sister all about dentists, how they looked after people's teeth for them, and made teeth for grown-up people who hadn't any of their own.

The window-cleaner man told my naughty little sister that *his* teeth were dentist-teeth and they were much prettier than his old ones, and my naughty little sister was very interested, and she said she would like the dentist to see her wiggly tooth.

So, the next time my mother said,

'What about that tooth, now?' my naughty little sister said, 'I want to go to the dentist.'

My mother said, 'Goodness me, surely it's loose enough for you to pull out yourself now?'

But my naughty little sister started to cry, 'I want to go the dentist. I want to go, I do,' in a miserable voice like that.

So my mother said, 'Very well then. I want the dentist to see your teeth anyway, so we shall go as soon as he can see you!'

Well now, the dentist was a very nice man, he said he thought he'd really better see my naughty little sister's tooth right away.

When my mother and my little sister arrived at the dentist's they had to wait in the waiting-room with a lot of other people. My naughty little sister told all these other people about her wiggly tooth, and she showed it to them, and they all said what a lucky child she was to have such a wiggly tooth.

When it was my naughty little sister's turn to see the dentist, she was very pleased. She sat on his big chair and let him have a good look.

The dentist said, 'It's a very nice tooth, old lady. I'm sorry you don't want it taken out.'

'I want it to wiggle with,' said my silly little sister. Then my little sister asked all about making teeth and everything, and the dentist told her very nicely.

'It's a pity you don't want to part with that tooth though,' he said, 'because I should just like a tooth like that for my collection. I collect really nice teeth,' the dentist said.

My naughty little sister thought and thought, and she couldn't help seeing how very nice it would be to have a tooth in a real collection, so, do you know what she did? She put her hand up to her mouth, as quick as quick, and then she said, 'Here you are,' and there, right in the middle of her hand was her little tooth. She'd pulled it out all her very self.

6. The fairy-doll

When I was a little girl, I had a fairy-doll that was so beautiful that I never wanted to play with it.

It had real shiny wings and a shiny crown and a fairy-wand, and a sticking-out dress with golden stars on it, and it shut its eyes when you laid it down and opened them when you stood it up, and said, 'ma-ma,' if you tipped it forwards.

It was so beautiful, that I kept it in its box, wrapped up in white paper, in the drawer of my mother's wardrobe. I

used to go and peep at it whenever I specially wanted to.

Well now, my naughty little sister had a doll too. Her doll was a very poor old thing, with no eyes left, and all its nose rubbed off. My naughty little sister called *her* doll 'Rosy-Primrose'. My little sister used to take Rosy-Primrose to bed with her, but sometimes, when my naughty little sister was cross, she would smack poor Rosy-Primrose and throw her out of bed.

One day, when my naughty little sister threw Rosy-Primrose out of bed, my mother said, 'I think I'll take that poor old doll downstairs and put her in the cupboard until you can be kind to her.'

But my naughty little sister said, 'Won't be kind to her.' So my mother put Rosy-Primrose away in the cupboard for a rest.

Now, what do you think? The very next day, when my mother was doing the ironing, she suddenly said, 'Where is that naughty little girl? Where is that naughty sister of yours? I expect she's in mischief, because she is so quiet.' That's what my mother said.

So my mother stopped her ironing, and went out into the garden to look for my little sister. But she wasn't in the garden. My mother looked in the shed, and she wasn't in the shed. She wasn't in the sitting-room, or in her bedroom, or in the spare room, but when my mother peeped into her own bedroom – there was my naughty little sister looking very cross at being caught.

The fairy-doll's box wasn't in the

wardrobe drawer either. It was *on the bed*, and all the white paper was all over the floor, and there was my naughty little sister holding my fairy-doll and making it say, 'ma-ma, ma-ma, ma-ma, ma-ma.'

My mother was very cross. She said, 'That's not your doll. It belongs to your big sister,' and my naughty little sister said, 'I want it.' My mother said, 'Put it down on the bed,' and my very naughty little sister said, 'No.'

Then my mother was angry, and went to take the doll away from my naughty little sister, but that bad child ran away with my lovely fairy-doll.

And, well – you remember what she did to poor Rosy-Primrose when she was cross, don't you? She did something *even more dreadful* to my fairy-doll. *She threw it out of the window*, that lovely beautiful doll with the golden wings and the shiny crown *and* the sticking-out dress with golden stars on.

My naughty little sister had to go straight to bed for that, because she really had been terrible.

My lovely fairy-doll had fallen down into the garden, right into a muddy puddle, and its face was broken. I cried and cried, and when

my little sister saw
the poor fairy-doll,
she cried and cried
too, because she
wasn't really such
a bad child as all
that – she just threw
the doll out of the window
when she was being mischievous.

My naughty little sister was so very
sorry that we all forgave her, and my
mother said that if she promised to be
kind in future, she should have Rosy-
Primrose back very soon. So my little
sister promised hard.

Do you know what my kind mother

did? She sent the poor fairy-doll to the Dolls' Hospital, and she sent Rosy-Primrose there too, and when the two dolls came back, they looked very nice.

My little sister was a bit sorry to see Rosy-Primrose, because Rosy-Primrose had a new nice face and some curly hair that hadn't been there for a long, long time. My little sister never was quite happy with the tidy Rosy-Primrose until it lost all its hair again, and its new eyes fell in. But she was always kind to it after that.

I was glad about my fairy-doll, though. Because it wasn't a fairy any more after the window-fall. It had a pretty new face, and a nice smile with teeth showing, and it *still* shut its eyes when you laid it down, and it *still* said, 'ma-ma'; but the fairy clothes had all been spoiled in the muddy puddle, so my mother had made it a nice yellow dress and bonnet, and a white apron, and I called it 'Annabella' and, now that its clothes were not so grand, I could play with it whenever I wanted to – so really that fairy-doll's window-fall wasn't so terribly dreadful after all.

7. My Naughty Little Sister
cuts out

Once, when I was a little girl, and my naughty little sister was a very little girl, it rained and rained and rained. It rained every day, and it rained all the time, and everything got wetter and wetter and wetter, and when my naughty little sister went out she had to wear her mackintosh and her wellingtons.

My naughty little sister had a beautiful red mackintosh-cape with a hood – just like Little Red Riding Hood's – and she had a little red umbrella.

My little sister used to carry her umbrella under her cape, because she didn't want it to get wet. Wasn't she a silly girl?

When my naughty little sister went down the road, the rain went plop, plop, plop, plop, on to her head, and scatter-scatter-scatter against her cape, and trickle, trickle down her cheeks, and her wellington boots went splish-splosh, splish-splosh in the puddles.

My naughty little sister liked puddles very much, and she splished and sploshed such a lot that the water

got into the tops of her wellingtons and made her feet wet inside, and then my naughty little sister was very sorry, because she caught a cold.

She got a nasty, sneezy, atishoo-y cold, and couldn't go out in the rain any more. My poor little sister looked very miserable when my mother said she could not go out. But her cold was very bad, and she had a red nose, and red eyes, and a nasty buzzy ear – all because of getting her feet wet, and every now and again – she couldn't help it – she said, 'A-a-tishoo!'

Now, my naughty little sister was a fidgety child. She wouldn't sit down quietly to hear a story like you do, or play nicely with a toy, or draw pictures with a pencil – she just fidgeted and wriggled and grumbled all the time, and said, 'Want to go out in the rain – want to splash and splash,' in the crossest and growliest voice, and then she said, 'A-a-tishoo!' even when she didn't want to, because of the nasty cold she'd got. And she grumbled and grumbled and grumbled.

My mother made her an orange-drink, but she grumbled. My mother gave her cough-stuff, but she grumbled, and really no one knew how to make her good.

My mother said, 'Why don't you look at a picture-book?'

And my naughty little sister said, 'No book, nasty book.'

Then my mother said, 'Well, would you like to play with my button-box?' and my naughty little sister said she thought she might like that. But when she had dropped all the buttons out and spilled them all over the floor, she said, 'No buttons, tired of buttons. A-a-tishoo!' She said, 'A-a-tishoo' like that, because she couldn't help it.

My mother said, 'Dear me, what can I do for the child?'

Then my mother had a good idea. She said, 'I know, you can make a scrap-book!'

So my mother found a big book with clean pages and a lot of old birthday cards and Christmas cards, and some old picture-books, and a big pot of sticky paste, and she showed my naughty little sister how to make a scrap-book.

My naughty little sister was quite pleased, because she had never been allowed to use scissors before, and these were the nice snippy ones from Mother's work-box.

My naughty little sister cut out a picture of a cow, and a basket with roses in, and a lady in a red dress, and a house and a squirrel, and she stuck them all in the big book with the sticky paste, and then she laughed and laughed.

Do you know why she laughed? She laughed because she had stuck them all in the book in a funny way. She stuck the lady in first, and then she put the basket of roses on the lady's head, and the cow on top of that, and then she put the house and the squirrel under the lady's feet. My naughty little sister thought that the lady looked very funny with the basket of flowers and the cow on her head.

So my naughty little sister amused herself for quite a long while, and my mother said, 'Thank goodness,' and went upstairs to tidy the bedrooms, as my naughty little sister wasn't grumbling any more.

But that naughty child soon got tired of the scrap-book, and when she got tired of it, she started rubbing all the sticky paste over the table and made the table all gummy. Wasn't that nasty of her?

Then she poked the scissors into the birthday cards and the Christmas cards, and made them look very ugly, and then, because she liked to do snip-snipping with the scissors, she looked round for something big to cut.

Fancy looking round for mischief like that! But she did. She didn't care at all, she just looked round for something to cut.

She snipped up all Father's newspaper with the scissors, and she tried to snip the pussy-cat's tail, only pussy put her back up and said 'Pss', and frightened my naughty little sister.

So my naughty little sister looked round for something that she could cut up easily, and she found a big brown-paper parcel on a chair – a parcel all tied up with white string.

My naughty little sister was so bad because she couldn't go out to play in the wet, that she cut the string of the parcel. She knew that she shouldn't but she didn't care a bit. She cut the string right through, and pulled it all off. She did that because she thought it would be nice to cut up all the brown paper that was round the parcel.

So she dragged the parcel on to the floor, and began to pull off the brown paper. But when the brown paper was off, my very naughty little sister found something inside that she thought would be much nicer to cut. It was a lovely piece of silky, rustly material with little flowers all over it – the sort of special stuff that party-dresses are made of.

Now, my naughty little sister knew that she mustn't cut stuff like that but she didn't care. She thought she would just make a quick snip to see how it sounded when it was cut. So she did make a snip, and the stuff went 'scc-scrr-scrr' as the scissors bit it, and my naughty little sister was so pleased that she forgot about everything else, and just cut and cut.

And then, all of a sudden . . . yes! *In came my mother!*

My mother was cross when she saw

the sticky table, and the cut-up newspaper, but when she looked on the floor and saw my naughty little sister cutting the silky stuff, she was very, very angry.

'You are a bad, bad child,' my mother said. 'You shall not have the scissors any more. Your kind Aunt Betty is going to be married soon, and she sent this nice stuff for me to make you a bridesmaid's dress, because she wanted you to hold up her dress in church for her. Now you won't be able to go.'

My naughty little sister cried and cried because she wanted to be a bridesmaid and because she liked to have new dresses very much. But it was no use, because the stuff was all cut up.

After that my naughty little sister tried to be a good girl until her cold was better.

8. My Naughty Little Sister at the party

You wouldn't think there could be another child as naughty as my naughty little sister, would you? But there was. There was a thoroughly bad boy who was my naughty little sister's best boy-friend, and this boy's name was Harry.

This Bad Harry and my naughty little sister used to play together quite a lot in Harry's garden, or in our garden, and got up to dreadful mischief between them, picking all the baby gooseberries, and the green blackcurrants, and throwing sand on the flower-beds, and digging up the runner-bean seeds, and all the naughty sorts of things you never, never do in the garden.

Now, one day this Bad Harry's birthday was near, and Bad Harry's mother said he could have a birthday-party and invite lots of children to tea. So Bad Harry came round to our house with a pretty card in an envelope for my naughty little sister, and this card was an invitation asking my naughty little sister to come to the birthday-party.

Bad Harry told my naughty little

sister that there would be a lovely tea with jellies and sandwiches and birthday-cake, and my naughty little sister said, 'Jolly good.'

And every time she thought about the party she said, 'Nice tea and birthday-cake.' Wasn't she greedy? And when the party day came she didn't make any fuss when my mother dressed her in her new green party-dress, and her green party-shoes and her green hair-ribbon, and she didn't fidget and she didn't wriggle her head about when she was having her hair combed, she kept as still as still, because she was so pleased to think about the party, and when my mother said, 'Now, what must you say at the party?' my naughty little sister said, 'I must say, "nice tea".'

But my mother said, 'No, no, that *would* be a greedy thing to say. You must say, "please" and "thank you" like a good polite child, at tea-time, and say, "thank you very much for having me", when the party is over.'

And my naughty little sister said, 'All right, Mother, I promise.'

So, my mother took my naughty little sister to the party, and what do you think the silly little girl did as soon as she got there? She went up to

Bad Harry's mother and she said very quickly, 'Please-and-thank-you, and thank-you-very-much-for-having-me,' all at once – just like that, before she forgot to be polite, and then she said, 'Now, may I have a lovely tea?'

Wasn't that rude and greedy? Bad Harry's mother said, 'I'm afraid you will have to wait until all the other children are here, but Harry shall show you the tea-table if you like.'

Bad Harry looked very smart in a blue party-suit, with white socks and shoes and a *real man's haircut*, and he said, 'Come on, I'll show you.'

So they went into the tea-room and

there was the birthday-tea spread out on the table. Bad Harry's mother had made red jellies and yellow jellies, and blancmanges and biscuits and sandwiches and cakes-with-cherries-on, and a big birthday-cake with white icing on it and candles and 'Happy Birthday Harry' written on it.

My naughty little sister's eyes grew bigger and bigger, and Bad Harry

said, 'There's something else in the larder. It's going to be a surprise treat, but you shall see it because you are my best girl-friend.'

So Bad Harry took my naughty little sister out into the kitchen and they took chairs and climbed up to the larder shelf – which is a dangerous thing to do, and it would have been their own faults if they had fallen down – and Bad Harry showed my naughty little sister a lovely spongy trifle, covered with creamy stuff and with silver balls and jelly-sweets on the top. And my naughty little sister stared more than ever because she liked spongy trifle better than jellies or blancmanges or biscuits or sandwiches or cakes-with-cherries-on, or even birthday-cake, so she said, 'For me.'

Bad Harry said, 'For me too,' because he liked spongy trifle best as well.

Then Bad Harry's mother called to them and said, 'Come along, the other children are arriving.'

So they went to say, 'How do you do!' to the other children, and then Bad Harry's mother said, 'I think we will have a few games now before tea – just until everyone has arrived.'

All the other children stood in a ring

and Bad Harry's mother said, 'Ring O'Roses first, I think.' And all the nice party children said, 'Oh, we'd like that.'

But my naughty little sister said, 'No Ring O'Roses – nasty Ring O'Roses' – just like that, because she didn't like Ring O'Roses very much, and Bad Harry said, 'Silly game.' So Bad Harry and my naughty little sister stood and watched the others. The other children sang beautifully too, they sang:

'Ring O'Ring O'Roses,
A pocket full of posies –
A-tishoo, a-tishoo, we all fall down.'

And they all fell down and laughed, but Harry and my naughty little sister didn't laugh. They got tired of watching and they went for a little walk. Do you know where they went to?

Yes. To the larder. To take another look at the spongy trifle. They climbed up on to the chairs to look at it really properly. It was very pretty.

'Ring O'Ring O'Roses' sang the good party children.

'Nice jelly-sweets,' said my naughty little sister. 'Nice silver balls,' and she looked at that terribly bad Harry and he looked at her.

'Take one,' said that naughty boy, and my naughty little sister did take one, she took a red jelly-sweet from the top of the trifle; and then Bad Harry took a green jelly-sweet; and then my naughty little sister took a yellow jelly-sweet and a silver ball, and then Bad Harry took three jelly-sweets, red,

green and yellow, and six silver balls. One, two, three, four, five, six, and put them all in his mouth at once.

Now some of the creamy stuff had come off on Bad Harry's finger and he liked it very much, so he put his finger into the creamy stuff on the trifle, and took some of it off and ate it, and my naughty little sister ate some too. I'm sorry to have to tell you this, because I feel so ashamed of them, and expect you feel ashamed of them too.

I hope you aren't too shocked to hear any more? Because, do you know, those two bad children forgot all about the party and the nice children all singing 'Ring O'Roses'. They took a spoon each and scraped off the creamy stuff and ate it, and then they began to eat the nice spongy inside.

Bad Harry said, 'Now we've made the trifle look so untidy, no one else will want any, so we may as well eat it all up.' So they dug away into the spongy inside of the trifle and found lots of nice fruit bits inside. It was a very big trifle, but those greedy children ate and ate.

Then, just as they had nearly finished the whole big trifle, the 'Ring O'Roses'-ing stopped, and Bad Harry's mother called, 'Where are you two?

We are ready for tea.'

Then my naughty little sister was very frightened. Because she knew she had been very naughty, and she looked at Bad Harry and *he* knew *he* had been very naughty, and they both felt terrible. Bad Harry had a creamy mess of trifle all over his face, and even in his real man's haircut, and my naughty little sister had made her new green party-dress all trifly – you know how it happens if you eat too quickly and greedily.

'It's tea-time,' said Bad Harry, and he looked at my naughty little sister, and my naughty little sister thought of the jellies and the cakes and the sandwiches, and all the other things, and she felt very full of trifle, and she said, 'Don't want any.'

And do you know what she did? Just as Bad Harry's mother came into the kitchen, my naughty little sister slipped out of the door, and ran and ran all the way home. It was a good thing our home was only down the street and no roads to cross, or I don't know what would have happened to her.

Bad Harry's mother was so cross when she saw the trifle, that she sent Bad Harry straight to bed, and he had to stay there and hear all the nice children enjoying themselves. I don't know what happened to him in the night, but I know that my naughty little sister wasn't at all a well girl, from having eaten so much trifle – and I also know that she doesn't like spongy trifle any more.

9. The naughtiest story of all

This is such a very terrible story about my naughty little sister that I hardly know how to tell it to you. It is all about one Christmas-time when I was a little girl, and my naughty little sister was a very little girl.

Now, my naughty little sister was very pleased when Christmas began to draw near, because she liked all the excitement of the plum-puddings and the turkeys, and the crackers and the holly, and all the Christmassy-looking shops, but there was one very awful thing about her – she didn't like to think about Father Christmas at all – she said he was a *horrid old man*!

There – I knew you would be shocked at that. But she did. And she said she wouldn't put up her stocking for him.

My mother told my naughty little sister what a good old man Father Christmas was, and how he brought the toys along on Christmas Eve, but my naughty little sister said, 'I don't care. And I don't want that nasty old man coming to our house.'

Well now, that was bad enough, wasn't it? But the really dreadful thing happened later on.

This is the dreadful thing: one day, my school-teacher said that a Father Christmas Man would be coming to the school to bring presents for all the children, and my teacher said that the Father Christmas Man would have toys for all our little brothers and sisters as well, if they cared to come along for them. She said that there would be a real Christmas tree with candles on it, and sweeties and cups of tea and biscuits for our mothers.

Wasn't that a nice thought? Well now, when I told my little sister about the Christmas tree, she said, 'Oh, nice!'

And when I told her about the sweeties she said, 'Very, very nice!' But when I told her about the Father Christmas Man, she said, 'Don't want *him*, nasty old man.'

Still, my mother said, 'You can't go to the Christmas tree without seeing him, so if you don't want to see him all that much, you will have to stay at home.'

But my naughty little sister did want to go, very much, so she said, 'I will go, and when the horrid Father Christmas Man comes in, I will close my eyes.'

So, we all went to the Christmas

tree together, my mother and I, and my naughty little sister.

When we got to the school, my naughty little sister was very pleased to see all the pretty paper-chains that we had made in school hung all round the class-rooms, and when she saw all the little lanterns, and the holly and all the robin-redbreast drawings pinned on the blackboards she smiled and smiled. She was very smiley at first.

All the mothers, and the little brothers and sisters who were too young for school sat down on chairs and desks, and all the big school-children acted a play for them.

My little sister was very excited to see all the children dressed up as fairies and robins and elves and bo-peeps and things, and she clapped her hands very hard, like all the grown-ups did, to show that she was enjoying herself. And she still smiled.

Then, when some of the teachers came round with bags of sweets, tied up in pretty coloured paper, my little sister smiled even more, and she sang too when all the children sang. She sang, 'Away in a Manger', because she knew the words very well.

When she didn't know the words of some of the singing, she 'la-la'd'.

After all the singing, the teachers put out the lights, and took away a big screen from a corner of the room, and there was the Christmas tree, all lit up with candles and shining with silvery stuff, and little shiny coloured balls. There were lots of toys on the tree, and all the children cheered and clapped.

Then the teachers put the lights on again, and blew out the candles, so that we could all go and look at the tree. My little sister went too. She looked at the tree, and she looked at the toys, and she saw a specially nice doll with a blue dress on, and she said, 'For me.'

My mother said, 'You must wait and see what you are given.'

Then the teachers called out, 'Back to your seats, everyone, we have a visitor coming.' So all the children went back to their seats, and sat still and waited and listened.

And, as we waited and listened, we heard a tinkle-tinkle bell noise, and then the schoolroom door opened, and in walked the Father Christmas Man. My naughty little sister had forgotten all about him, so she hadn't time to close her eyes before he walked in.

However, when she saw him, my little sister stopped smiling and began to be stubborn.

The Father Christmas Man was very nice. He said he hoped we were having a good time, and we all said, 'Yes,' except my naughty little sister – she didn't say a thing.

Then he said, 'Now, one at a time, children; and I will give each one of you a toy.'

So, first of all each school-child went up for a toy, and my naughty little sister still didn't shut her eyes because she wanted to see who was going to have the specially nice doll in the blue dress. But none of the school-children had it.

Then Father Christmas began to call the little brothers and sisters up for presents, and, as he didn't know their names, he just said, 'Come along, sonny,' if it were a boy, and 'come along, girlie,' if it were a girl. The Father Christmas Man let the little brothers and sisters choose their own toys off the tree.

When my naughty little sister saw this, she was so worried about the specially nice doll, that she thought that she would just go up and get it. She said, 'I don't like that horrid old beardy man, but I do like that nice doll.'

So, my naughty little sister got up without being asked to, and she went right out to the front where the Father Christmas Man was standing, and she said, 'That doll, please,' and pointed to the doll she wanted.

The Father Christmas Man laughed and all the teachers laughed, and the other mothers and the school-children, and all the little brothers and sisters. My mother did not laugh because she was so shocked to see my naughty little sister going out without being asked to.

The Father Christmas Man took the specially nice doll off the tree, and he handed it to my naughty little sister and he said, 'Well now, I hear you don't like me very much, but won't you just shake hands?' and my naughty little sister said, 'No.' But she took the doll all the same.

The Father Christmas Man put out his nice old hand for her to shake and be friends, and do you know what that naughty bad girl did? *She bit his hand.* She really and truly did. Can you think of anything more dreadful and terrible? She bit Father Christmas's good old hand, and then she turned and ran and ran out of the school with all the children staring after her, and her doll held very tight in her arms.

The Father Christmas Man was very nice, he said it wasn't a hard bite, only a frightened one, and he made all the children sing songs together.

When my naughty little sister was brought back by my mother, she said she was very sorry, and the Father Christmas Man said, 'That's all right, old lady,' and because he was so smiley and nice to her, my funny little sister went right up to him, and gave him a big 'sorry' kiss, which pleased

him very much.

And she hung her stocking up after all, and that kind man remembered to fill it for her.

My naughty little sister kept the specially nice doll until she was quite grown-up. She called it Rosy-Primrose, and although she was sometimes bad-tempered with it, she really loved it very much indeed.

10. My Naughty Little Sister does knitting

One day, when I was a little girl, and my naughty little sister was another little girl, a kind lady came to live next door to us. This kind lady's really true name was Mrs Jones, but my little sister always called her Mrs Cocoa Jones.

Do you know why she called her that? Shall I tell you? *Well*, it was because Mrs Cocoa Jones used to give my naughty little sister a cup of cocoa every morning.

Yes, every single morning, when it

was eleven o'clock, Mrs Cocoa Jones used to bang hard on her kitchen wall with the handle of her floor-brush, and as our kitchen was right the other side of the wall, my naughty little sister could hear very well, and would bang and bang back to show that she was quite ready.

Then, my little sister would go into Mrs Cocoa Jones's house to drink cocoa with her. Wasn't that a nice idea?

My little sister used to go in to see Mrs Cocoa Jones so much that Mr Cocoa Jones made a little low gate between his garden and our father's garden so that my little sister could pop in without having to go all round the front of the houses each time. Mr Cocoa Jones made a nice little archway over the gate, and planted a little rose-tree to climb over it, especially for her. Wasn't she a fortunate child?

So you see, Mrs Cocoa Jones was a very great friend.

Well now, Mrs Cocoa Jones was a lady who was always knitting and knitting, and as she hadn't any little boys and girls of her own, she used to knit a lot of lovely woollies for my naughty little sister, and for me.

She knitted us red jumpers and blue jumpers, and yellow jumpers and red caps and blue caps and yellow caps to match, and she also knitted a blue jumper for Rosy-Primrose, who was my naughty little sister's favourite doll, and when she had finished all the caps and jumpers, she made us lots of pairs of socks. So, every time we saw Mrs Cocoa, she always had a bag of wool and a lot of clicky needles.

Sometimes, when Mrs Cocoa Jones wanted the wool wound up, she would ask my naughty little sister to hold it for her, and that fidgety child would drop it and tangle it, until Mr Cocoa

Jones used to say, 'It looks to me as if you will be doing knotting not knitting with that lot,' to Mrs Cocoa. And my funny little sister would laugh and laugh because she thought it was very funny to say 'knotting' like that.

Now, one day Mrs Cocoa Jones said, 'Would you like to learn to knit?' to my naughty little sister.

'Would you like to learn to knit?' she asked my little sister, and my little sister said, 'Not very much.'

Then Mrs Cocoa Jones said, 'Well, but think of all the nice things you could make for everyone. You could knit Christmas presents and birthday presents all by yourself.'

Then my naughty little sister thought it would be rather nice to learn to knit, so she said, 'All right then, Mrs Cocoa Jones, would you please teach me?'

So Mrs Cocoa Jones lent her a pair of rather bendy needles and she gave her some wool, and she showed her how to knit. So, carefully, carefully my little sister learned to put the wool round the needle, and carefully, carefully to bring it out and make a stitch, and carefully, carefully to make another until she could really truly knit.

Then my naughty little sister was very pleased, because she had a good idea. She thought that as Mr Cocoa Jones had made her such a nice little gate, she would knit him a new scarf for his birthday, because his old scarf had got all moth-holey. The naughty little baby moths had eaten bits of scarf and made holes in it, so my little sister thought he would like a new one very much.

She didn't tell anyone about it. Not even Mrs Cocoa Jones, she wanted it to be a real secret.

Well now, Mrs Cocoa had given my little sister all her odds and endsy bits of wool, and the red bits and the blue bits and the yellow bits from our jumpers, and some grey and purple and white and black and brown bits as well, so my little sister thought she would make a beautiful scarf.

She went secretly, secretly into corners to knit this beautiful scarf for Mr Cocoa Jones's birthday. Wasn't she a clever child?

She kept it carefully hidden all the time she wasn't making it. She hid it in lots of funny places too. She hid it under her pillow, and in the coal-shed and behind the settee, and in the flour-tub. But most of the time she was knitting and knitting to have it made in time. So that, when Mr Cocoa Jones's birthday did come, it was quite ready and quite finished.

It was a very pretty scarf because of all the pretty colours my little sister had used, and although it was a bit coaly and a bit floury here and there, it still looked very lovely, and Mr Cocoa Jones was very pleased with it.

He said, 'It's the best scarf I have ever had!'

Then my little sister told him all

about how she had knitted it, and she showed him some holes in it too, where the stitches had dropped, and Mr Cocoa Jones said they would make nice homes for the baby moths to live in anyway, so my little sister was glad she had dropped the stitches.

Then Mr Cocoa Jones said that as it was the very nicest scarf he had ever had knitted for him, it would be a shame to waste it by wearing it every day. So he said he would get Mrs Cocoa to put it away for him for High Days and Holidays.

So Mrs Cocoa wrapped it up very neatly and nicely in blue laundry paper, and she let my little sister put it away in Mr Cocoa's drawer for him, and Mr Cocoa wore his old scarf for every day until Mrs Cocoa had time to knit him another one.

11. My Naughty Little Sister goes to the pantomime

A long time ago, when I was a little girl, and my little sister was a little girl too, my mother took us to see the Christmas Pantomime.

The Pantomime was in a Theatre, which was a very beautiful place with red tippy-up seats and a lot of ladies and gentlemen playing music in front of the curtains.

My little sister was a very good quiet child at first, because she had never been to the Pantomime before. She sat very still and mousy. She didn't say anything. She just looked and looked.

She looked at the lights, and the lots and lots of seats, and the music-people, and the other boys and girls. She didn't even fidget at first, because she wasn't quite sure about the tippy-up seat.

When we were in the Theatre, our mother gave us a bag of sweets each. I had chocolate-creams, and my little sister had toffee-drops, because she liked them so much, but she was so quiet that she didn't eat even a single one of them before the Pantomime started.

She just held the sweeties on her

lap, so that when the music man who plays the cymbals suddenly made them go 'Rish-tish a-tish!' and the curtains came back, she was so surprised that she dropped them all over the floor, and my mother had to pick them up for her.

My little sister was so surprised

because she hadn't known that Pantomime was people dancing and singing and falling over things, but when she saw that it was, she was very excited, and when the other children clapped their hands, she clapped hers very hard too.

At first, my little sister was so surprised that she liked every bit of it, but after a while she said her favourite was the fat funny man. The play was all about the Babes in the Wood, and the fat funny man was called Humpty Dumpty. He was very very funny indeed, and when he came on, he always said, 'Hallo, boys and girls.'

And the boys and girls said, 'Hallo, Humpty Dumpty.'

And he said, 'How are you tomorrow?' and we said, 'We are very well today.' He told us to say this every time, and we never forgot. Once, my little sister shouted so loud, *'Hallo, Humpty Dumpty,'* – she shouted 'HALLO, HUMPTY DUMPTY,' – like that, that Humpty Dumpty heard her, and he waved specially to her. My goodness, wasn't she a proud girl then.

The other thing my little sister liked was the fairies dancing. There were lots of fairies in the Pantomime, and they had lovely sparkly dresses, and

when they danced the lights went red
and blue and green, and some of them
really flew right up in the air!

Humpty Dumpty tried to fly too,
but he fell right over and bumped his
nose. My naughty little sister was so
sorry for him, that she began to cry
and cry, really true tear-crying, not
just howling.

But when Humpty Dumpty jumped up and said, 'Hallo, boys and girls,' and we all said, 'Hallo, Humpty Dumpty,' and when he began to dance again, she knew he wasn't really hurt so she laughed and laughed.

And presently, what do you think? My little sister had a really exciting thing happen.

Humpty Dumpty came on the stage and he sang a little song for all the boys and girls, and then he made all the children sing too. After that he said, 'Would any little boy or girl like to come up on the stage and dance with me?' And do you know what, my little sister said, 'Yes. I will. I will.' And she ran out of her seat and up the stage steps and right on to the big theatre stage before my mother could do anything about it.

All the people cheered and clapped when my little sister ran up on to the stage, and a lot of other boys and girls went up too then, and soon they were all dancing with Humpty Dumpty. Round and round and up and down, until two ladies dressed like men came on the stage.

Then Humpty Dumpty said, 'All right, children, down you go,' and all the boys and girls went down again, off the stage and back to their mothers.

All except my bad little sister. *Because she wasn't there.* She'd vanished! And what do you think?

While the two ladies dressed like men were singing on the stage, the funny man came back, with my little sister sitting on his shoulder. And he came right off the stage and down the steps and brought her back to Mother, and my little sister looked very pleased and smiley.

All the people stared and stared to see my naughty little sister carried back by Humpty Dumpty. Even the singing ladies dressed like men stared.

And do you know where she had been?

The bad child had slipped round the side of the stage while the other children were dancing, to see if she could find the fairies!

And she did find them too. She said they were drinking lemonade and they gave her some as well. It wasn't very fairyish lemonade, she said, it was the fizzy nose-tickle sort.

She told us another thing too, a secret thing. She said they weren't real true fairies, only little girls like herself, and she said that when she was a bit older, she was going to be a stage fairy like those little girls.

12. My Naughty Little Sister goes to school

One day, when I was a little girl, my mother had a letter from my grannie, to say that she was ill in bed, and would Mother come over for a day to see her?

So my mother wrote a letter to my school-teacher to ask if my little sister could come to school with me next day, as Grannie was ill. My teacher said, 'Yes, she can come if she will be good.' And wasn't my funny little sister pleased.

Do you know what she did? She

found an old case belonging to my father, and she put in it all the things she thought she would want for school next day. She put in a pencil and rubber, and some crayons and some story-books, and an apple and a matchbox, and Rosy-Primrose who was her doll.

Then she went to bed very quickly like a good girl. She didn't splash about in the bath, or scream when she had her hair done, or grumble about her supper, or say her prayers naughtily, or worry and worry for lots of stories in bed. No. She shut her eyes quickly so as to go to sleep and make tomorrow come as soon as soon. That's what the sensible child did.

And in the morning, she got up early, and she *dressed herself*. Yes! Even the *buttons*, and her socks! To show the teacher how nicely she could do it. Then, while our mother was getting the breakfast ready, she went out into the garden, and she picked a nice bunch of flowers out of her own garden for the teacher. So for once in a while she was my good little sister.

Well now, when my little sister got to school, she was still being very good. She said, 'Good morning,' to everyone and she came nicely into school, and because she looked so good and special the teacher said she could sit next to me all day.

So my little sister sat down right next to me, and stared and stared at all the other children in the room, and when she saw them opening their bags and cases and getting out their books and pencil-boxes, she opened her case and took out all her things too. She took out the pencil and the rubber, and the crayons and the story-books but she left the apple and the matchbox and Rosy-Primrose in the case because she wanted them for play-time.

When school started, my little sister

stood up very straight to sing the school hymns, and she shut her eyes very tight for the school prayers, and then she sat down as good as good, nice and straight like the teacher told us to.

Then the teacher called all the children's names, and when each child's name was called, the child said, 'Present'. My naughty little sister was very surprised, and when my name was called I said, 'Present' too. But the teacher didn't call my little sister's name, because she wasn't a real school-child, and do you know what my naughty little sister did?

She forgot to be a good child, and she started to shout, 'I want a present, I want a present.' Wasn't she silly?

But after that my little sister was very good again, and the teacher let her play with some plasticine. My little sister made a red basket with the plasticine, and the teacher said it was very good, and put it on the mantelpiece for everyone to see.

Then our teacher read us a story, and my little sister was very interested, and when our teacher asked questions about the story, and all the children put their hands up, my little sister put her hand up too, and all the children

laughed. But our teacher said they mustn't laugh, and she asked my little sister a real big-child's question about the story, and my little sister gave the *right answer*. Then our teacher said, as my little sister was such a clever child she could have ten out of ten. You know ten out of ten is a very big thing to have at school.

So our teacher wrote, 'Ten out of ten' on a piece of paper for my little sister and put it on the mantelpiece for her with the plasticine basket, and my little sister was a very proud child.

When dinner-time came, our teacher let my little sister sit with her, and my little sister was so good that the teacher said all the other children should try to be like her. Wasn't she behaving well?

In the afternoon we all drew pictures with our crayons, and my little sister drew a picture with her crayons. She was very pleased to think she had brought her own crayons to school.

I drew a little house, and a tree and a pond, and some little people. But do you know what my little sister drew? She drew the teacher, and all the school-children! Yes, all of them in the class. The teacher was very pleased to see such a lovely drawing, because my little sister had not forgotten anything – she had even put in her plasticine basket and her ten out of ten writing. So teacher said the drawing must go on the mantelpiece with the other clever things. My little sister drew in her drawing very small next to the plasticine basket, and then the picture was put up for everyone to see.

Then we all went out into the playground and did drill, and my little sister did drill as well, and she stood so straight, and put her arms so nicely that teacher let her do it in front of all the class.

So you see, she was being a very good child.

When we went back into school though, and did reading, my little sister got very quiet, and very still, and do you know what happened? She fell fast asleep on the desk. She slept and

slept right until our mother came
to fetch us home, and, because she
had been so good and no trouble,
our teacher let her take home the
lovely drawing, and the plasticine
basket, and the ten out of ten paper.

13. When my father minded my Naughty Little Sister

When my sister was a naughty little girl, she had a very cross friend. My little sister's cross friend was called Mr Blakey, and he was a very grumbly old man.

My little sister's friend Mr Blakey was the shoe-mender man, and he had a funny little shop with bits of leather all over the floor, and boxes of nails, and boot-polish, and shoe-laces, all over the place. Mr Blakey had a picture in his shop too. It was a very beautiful picture of a dog with boots on all four feet, walking in the rain. My little sister loved that picture very much, but she loved Mr Blakey better than that.

Every time we went in Mr Blakey's shop with our mother, my naughty little sister would start meddling with things, and Mr Blakey would say, 'Leave that be, you varmint,' in a very loud cross voice, and my little sister would stop meddling at once, just like an obedient child, because Mr Blakey was her favourite man, and one day, when we went into his shop, do you know what she did? She went straight behind the counter and kissed him *without being asked.* Mr Blakey was very surprised because he had a lot of nails in his mouth, but after that, he always gave her a peppermint humbug after he had shouted at her.

Well, that's about Mr Blakey in case you wonder who he was later on, now this is the real story:

One day, my mother had to go out shopping, so she asked my father if he would mind my naughty little sister for the day. My mother said she would take me shopping because I was a big girl, but my little sister was too draggy and moany to go to the big shops.

My father said he would mind my

little sister, but my little sister said, 'I want to go, I want to go.' You know how she said that by now, I think. 'I want to go' – like that. And she kicked and screamed.

My mother said, 'Oh, dear, how tiresome you are,' to my little sister, but my father said, 'You'll jolly well do as you're told, old lady.'

Then my naughty little sister wouldn't eat her breakfast, but my mother went off shopping with me just the same, and when we had gone, my father looked very fierce, and he said, 'What about that breakfast?'

So my naughty little sister ate all

her breakfast up, every bit, and she said, 'More milk, please,' and 'more bread, please,' so much that my father got tired getting it for her.

Then, as it was a hot day, my father said, 'I'll bring my work into the garden, and give an eye to you at the same time.'

So my father took a chair and a table out into the garden, and my little sister went out into the garden too, and because my father was there she played good child's games. She didn't tread on the baby seedlings, or pick the flowers, or steal the blackcurrants, or do anything at all wicked. She didn't want my father to look fierce again, and my father said she was a good nice child.

My little sister just sat on the lawn and played with Rosy-Primrose, and she made a tea-party with leaves and nasturtium seeds, and when she wanted something she asked my father for it nicely, not going off and finding it for herself at all.

She said, 'Please, Father, would you get me Rosy-Primrose's box?' and my father put down his pen, and his writing-paper, and got out of his chair, and went and got Rosy-Primrose's box, which was on the top shelf of the toy-cupboard and had all Rosy-Primrose's tatty old clothes in it.

Then my father did writing again,

and then my little sister said, 'Please can I have a drink of water?' She said it nicely, 'Please,' she said.

That was very good of her to ask, because she sometimes used to drink germy water out of the water-butt, but Father wasn't pleased at all, he said, 'Bother!' because he was being a busy man, and he stamped and stamped to the kitchen to get the water for my polite little sister.

But my father didn't know about Rosy-Primrose's water. You see, when my little sister had a drink she always gave Rosy-Primrose a drink too in a blue doll's cup. So when my father brought back the water, my little sister said, 'Where is Rosy-Primrose's water?' and my cross father said, 'Bother Rosy-Primrose,' like that, cross and grumbly.

And my father was crosser and grumblier when my little sister asked him to put Rosy-Primrose's box back in the toy-cupboard, he said, 'That wretched doll again?' and he took Rosy-Primrose and shut her in the box too, and put it on top of the book-case, to show how firm he was going to be. So then my little sister stopped being good.

She started to yell and stamp, and make such a noise that people going by looked over the hedge to see what the matter was. Wouldn't you have been ashamed if it were you stamping and yelling with people looking at you? My naughty little sister wasn't ashamed. *She* didn't care about the people at all, she was a stubborn bad child.

My father was a stubborn man too. He took his table and his chair and his writing things indoors and shut himself away in his study. 'You'll jolly well stay there till you behave,' he said to my naughty little sister.

My naughty little sister cried and cried until my father looked out of the window and said, 'Any more of that, and off to bed you go.' Then she was quiet, because she didn't want to go to bed.

She only peeped in once after that, but my father said, 'Go away, do,' and went on writing and writing, and he was so interested in his writing, he forgot all about my little sister, and it wasn't until he began to get hungry that he remembered her at all.

Then my father went out into the kitchen, and there was a lot of nice salad-stuff in the kitchen that our mother had left for lunch, there was junket too, and stewed pears, and biscuits for my father and my little sister's lunches. My father remembered my little sister then, and he went to call her for lunch, because it was quite late. It was so late it was *four o'clock.*

But my little sister wasn't in the garden. My father looked and looked. He looked among the marrows, and behind the runner-bean rows, and under the hedge. He looked in the shed and down the cellar-hole, but there was no little girl.

Then my father went indoors again

and looked all over the house, and all the time he was calling and calling, but there was still no little girl at all.

Then my father got worried. He didn't stop to change his slippers or eat his lunch. He went straight out of the gate, and down the road to look for my little sister. But he couldn't see her at all. He asked people, 'Have you seen a little girl with red hair?' and people said, 'No.'

My father was just coming up the road again, looking so hot and so worried, when my mother and I got off the bus. When my mother saw him, she said, 'He's lost that child,' because she knows my father and my little sister rather well.

When we got indoors my mother said, 'Why haven't you eaten your lunch?' and then my father told her all about the writing, and my bad sister. So my mother said, 'Well, if she's anywhere, she's near food of some kind, have you looked in the larder?' My father said he had. So Mother said, 'Well, I don't know –'

Then I said something clever, I said, 'I expect she is with old Mr Blakey.' So we went off to Mr Blakey's shop, and there she was. Fast asleep on a pile of leather bits.

Mr Blakey seemed quite cross with us for having lost her, and my naughty little sister was very cross when we took her away because she said she had had a lovely time with Mr Blakey. Mr Blakey had boiled her an egg in his tea-kettle, and given her some bread and cheese out of newspaper, and let her cut it for herself with one of his nice leathery knives. Mother was cross because she had been looking forward to a nice cup of tea after the bus journey, and I was cross because my little sister had had such a fine time in Mr Blakey's shop.

The only happy one was my father. He said, 'Thank goodness I can work again without having to concentrate on a disagreeable baby.' However, that made my little sister cry again, so he wasn't happy for long.

14. My Naughty Little Sister and the good polite child

Once, a long time ago, when I was little, my mother said to my naughty little sister, 'I have a little girl coming to tea this afternoon. I hope you will be good and kind to her, because I am going to mind her while her mother goes out.'

My little sister was very interested about this little girl, and my mother said, 'Her name is Winnie and she is a good polite child, I hear.'

So my little sister got all her toys out and put them in the garden to show Winnie when she came, and my mother made some cherry cakes and jam-tarts, and some ginger biscuits for tea.

Wasn't my mother a kind woman, making those nice things for tea? Do you know, because Winnie was coming, my mother said, 'We will have tea in the garden, with the best bluebird tablecloth.'

My little sister liked this, because the bluebird tablecloth was very special. It had bluebirds on it, and trees on it, and little funny men walking on bridges on it, and little boats with men fishing on it, and they were all blue as blue. My little sister said, 'I shall like that.'

When it was time for Winnie to come, my mother changed my little sister's dress, and put on her a pair of nice blue socks. My little sister was very proud of those blue socks, and when she heard the knock on the front door she ran to show them to the good polite Winnie.

But what do you think? Winnie had blue socks too! And a blue silky dress, and blue shiny shoes, and when she came in, her mother put her a frilly white silky apron on to keep her dress clean. My little sister was so pleased to see how pretty Winnie looked that she forgot to say, 'How do you do?' She said, 'Blue socks too!' instead.

But do you know, that Winnie didn't say anything! She just stood and stood, and she didn't look at our mother, or my little sister, she just peeped. She made her eyes all peepy and small, because she didn't like to look at anyone, and when her mother went away, she didn't scream for her, or shout, 'Goodbye,' to her, or make any noise and fuss of any kind. She just went on being thoroughly peepy, and she went quietly, quietly into the garden with my little sister without saying anything at all.

My little sister showed Winnie all her toys. She showed her Rosy-Primrose first. Rosy-Primrose wasn't very beautiful that day, because it was a time when she had lost her hair and her eyes, and Winnie just peeped at Rosy-Primrose and didn't say anything.

So my little sister showed her the bricks, and the story-books and the teddies and the patty tins, and the tea-set and the jigsaws, and all the other

toys, and the good polite child didn't
say anything at all.

So my funny little sister said, 'Can
you talk?' and then Winnie said, 'Yes,'
to show she could speak, so my little
sister said, 'Would you like to make
mud-pies?'

That good Winnie said, 'Oh, no,
I might get dirty.' She didn't say

'Yes' because she didn't want to get her beautiful dress and her beautiful apron dirty, so my little sister said, 'Well, shall we go down the garden and eat gooseberries?' even though she knew that was naughty.

But good Winnie said, 'No, I might get tummy-ache.'

So my little sister said, 'Shall we have a race round the lawn?' and Winnie said, 'Oh, no, it's *so* hot,' in a quiet good voice.

And she didn't want to climb up the apple trees in case she tore her frock, and she didn't want to sit on the grass in case there were ants, and she didn't want to shout over the front gate to the school-children because it was rude, and all the time she just looked peepy, peepy at my little sister.

So then my little sister said, 'What would you like to do?' And the polite good Winnie said she would like to take a story-book indoors to read. So she took one of the story-books indoors and read it on her own.

My naughty little sister didn't want to read story-books indoors, so she went and made a dirt pie, and ate some gooseberries, and raced round the lawn, and climbed the apple trees, and sat on the grass, and then she shouted over the gate at the school-children, just to show how bad she could be.

When tea-time came, with all the nice cherry cakes and jam-tarts and ginger biscuits, the good polite Winnie came out and sat in the garden. When my little sister showed her the bluebird tablecloth Winnie only peeped and said, 'My mother has a tablecloth with roses and pansies and forget-me-nots on.'

And when my mother asked her to have a cake, she said, 'No, thank you, bread and butter, please,' and she wouldn't have a jam-tart, she had one little ginger biscuit, and then she said she wasn't hungry any more. Wasn't she polite?

My little sister wasn't polite like that. She had four cakes and three jam-tarts, and eight ginger biscuits. One, two, three, four, five, six, seven, eight, like that – and she ate them all, all up.

After tea good polite Winnie's mother came to fetch her home. She took off Winnie's apron and Winnie said, 'Good-bye, and thank you for minding me,' in a quiet good voice like that, 'Good afternoon,' she said.

And when she had gone, my mother said, 'What a quiet child.' But what do you think my funny little sister said? She said, 'I'm glad I'm not as good as all that.'

And my mother said, 'Oh, well, you are not so bad, I suppose.'

15. My Naughty Little Sister and the workmen

When my sister was a naughty little girl, she was a very, very inquisitive child. She was always looking and peeping into things that didn't belong to her. She used to open other people's cupboards and boxes just to find out what was inside.

Aren't you glad you aren't inquisitive like that?

Well now, one day a lot of workmen came to dig up all the roads near our house, and my little sister was very interested in them. They were very nice men, but some of them had rather loud shouty voices sometimes. There were shovelling men, and picking men, and men with jumping-about things that went 'Ah-ah-ah-ah-ah-ah-aha-aaa', and men who drank tea out of jam-pots, and men who cooked sausages over fires, and there was an old, old man who sat up all night when the other men had gone home, and who had a lot of coats and scarves to keep him warm.

There were lots of things for my little inquisitive sister to see, there were heaps of earth, and red lanterns for the old, old man to light at night-time,

and long pole-y things to keep people
from falling down the holes in the road,
and the workmen's huts, and many
other things.

When the workmen were in our
road, my little sister used to watch
them every day. She used to lean over
the gate and stare and stare, but when
they went off to the next road she didn't
see so much of them.

Well now, I will tell you about the
inquisitive thing my naughty little

sister did one day, shall I?

Yes. Well, do you remember Bad Harry who was my little sister's best boy-friend. Do you? I thought you did. Now this Bad Harry came one day to ask my mother if my little sister could go round to his house to play with him, and as Bad Harry's house wasn't far away, and as there were no roads to cross, my mother said my little sister could go.

So my little sister put on her hat and her coat, and her scarf and her gloves, because it was a cold nasty day, and went off with her best boy-friend to play with him.

They hurried along like good children until they came to the workmen in the next road, and then they went slow as slow, because there were so many things to see. They looked at this and at that, and when they got past the workmen they found a very curious thing.

By the road there was a tall hedge, and under the tall hedge there was a mackintoshy bundle.

Now this mackintoshy bundle hadn't anything to do with Bad Harry, and it hadn't anything to do with my naughty little sister, yet, do you know they were so inquisitive that they stopped and looked at it.

They had such a good look at it that they had to get right under the hedge to see, and when they got very near it they found it was an old mackintosh wrapped round something or other inside.

Weren't they naughty? They should have gone straight home to Bad Harry's mother's house, shouldn't they? But they didn't. They stayed and looked at the mackintoshy bundle.

And they opened it. They really truly did. It wasn't their bundle, but they opened it wide under the hedge, and do you know what was inside it?

I know you aren't an inquisitive meddlesome child, but would you like to know?

Well, inside the bundle there were lots and lots of parcels and packages tied up in red handkerchiefs, and brown paper, and newspaper, and instead of putting them back again like nice children, those little horrors started to open all those parcels, and inside those parcels there were lots of things to eat!

There were sandwiches, and cakes and meat-pies and cold cooked fish, and eggs, and goodness knows what-all.

Weren't those bad children surprised? They couldn't think how all those sandwiches and things could have got into the old mackintosh.

Then Bad Harry said, 'Shall we eat some?' You remember he was a greedy lad. But my little sister said, 'No, it's picked-up-food.' My little sister knew that my mother had told her never, never to eat picked-up-food. You see she was good about *that*.

Only she was very bad after that, because she said, 'I know, let's play with it.'

So they took out all those sandwiches and cakes and meat-pies

and cold cooked fish and eggs, and they laid them out across the path and made them into pretty patterns on the ground. Then Bad Harry threw a sandwich at my little sister and she threw a meat-pie at him, and they began to have a lovely game.

And then, do you know what happened? A big roary voice called out, 'WHAT ARE YOU DOING WITH OUR DINNERS, YOU MONKEYS – YOU?' And there was a big workman coming towards them, looking so cross and angry that those two bad children screamed and screamed, and because the workman was so roary, they turned and ran and ran back down the road, and the big

workman ran after them as cross as cross. Weren't they frightened?

When they got back to where the other roadmen were digging, those children were more frightened than ever, because the big workman shouted to all the workmen all about what those naughty children had done with their dinners.

Yes, those poor workmen had put all their dinners under the hedge in the old mackintosh to keep them dry and safe until dinner-time. As well as being frightened, Bad Harry and my naughty little sister were very ashamed.

They were so ashamed that they did a most silly thing. When they heard the big workman telling the others about their dinners, those silly children ran and hid themselves in one of the pipes that the workmen were putting in the road.

My naughty little sister went first, and old Bad Harry after her. Because my naughty little sister was so frightened she wriggled in and in the pipe, and Bad Harry came wriggling after her, because he was frightened too.

And then a dreadful thing happened to my naughty little sister.

That Bad Harry *stuck in the pipe* – and he couldn't get any farther. He was quite a round fat boy, you see, and he stuck fast as fast in the pipe.

Then didn't those sillies howl and howl.

My little sister howled because she didn't want to go on and on down the roadmen's pipes on her own, and Bad Harry howled because he couldn't move at all.

It was all terrible of course, but the roary workman rescued them very quickly. He couldn't reach Bad Harry with his arm, but he got a long hooky iron thing, and he hooked it in Bad

Harry's belt, and he pulled and pulled, and presently he pulled Bad Harry out of the pipe. Wasn't it a good thing they had the hooky iron? And wasn't it a very good thing that Bad Harry had a strong belt on his coat?

When Bad Harry was out, my little sister wriggled back and back, and came out too, and when she saw all the poor workmen who wouldn't have any dinner, she cried and cried, and she told them what a sorry girl she was. She told the workmen that she and Bad Harry hadn't known the mackintoshy bundle was their dinners, and Bad Harry said he was sorry too, and they were so really truly ashamed that the big workman said, 'Well, never mind this time. It's pay-day today, so we can all send the boy for fish and chips instead.' And he told my little sister not to cry any more.

So my little sister stopped crying, and she and Bad Harry both said they would never, never meddle and be inquisitive again.

My Naughty Little Sister's Friends

Contents

1. The Cocoa week-end

When I was a little girl I sometimes went to stay with my godmother-aunt in the country, for the week-end.

My mother would pack a little case for me, and then my godmother would come to spend a day with us and take me back with her.

My little sister was always very interested when she saw Mother packing my case, and she would remember things to go in it, and go and fetch them *without being asked*.

She used to ask me questions and

questions about going visiting, and when I told her everything she used to ask me all over again because she liked hearing it so much.

I told her about the nice little blue bed that I slept in at my godmother's and the picture of the big dog and the little dog on the bedroom wall. I told her and told her about them.

Then she wanted to hear about the things we had to eat and the things I did. I told her about all the tiny little baby-looking cakes that my godmother made, and about my godmother's piano, and how she let me play little made-up tunes on it if I wanted to.

And she would say, 'Tell me again about the piano,' my little sister would say. 'Tell me again. I like about the piano.'

So I would tell her about the piano all over again, and then I would pretend to play tunes on the table, and my sister would pretend to play tunes on the table too, and we would laugh and laugh.

But, when my mother said, 'Wouldn't you like to go on a visit one day?' my little sister would say, 'I'm not very sure.'

My little sister told her friend Mrs

Cocoa all about my goings away, and Mrs Cocoa was surprised to find how much my little sister knew about it, and she said, 'Wouldn't you like to go on a visit one day?' as well.

When Mrs Cocoa said this, my sister said, 'I don't think I should mind the visit but I shouldn't like the long-way-away.'

My little sister said, 'I should like to sleep in a different bed with a different picture on the wall and eat different dinners and play the piano, but I don't think I should like to go a long way to do it.'

You see my godmother-aunt did live

quite a long way from our house, and my little sister was rather frightened to think what a long way it was.

Now kind Mrs Cocoa thought about what my little sister had said, and the next time she heard that I was going to stay with my godmother-aunt, she said to my little sister, 'How would you like to go away for a week-end, too? How would you like to come and stay with me?'

Mrs Cocoa said, 'You can sleep in my little spare bedroom and eat all your dinners and things with Mr Cocoa and me, and you won't be a long-way-away, will you?'

Wasn't that a lovely idea for clever Mrs Cocoa to have had? Mrs Cocoa lived next door to us, and my little sister knew her house very well, but she had never slept there and had all her dinners and things there, so it would be a real visit, wouldn't it?

My sister was very pleased. It was just what she wanted: a real visit that was not far away, so she said at once, 'Please, Mrs Cocoa, I should like that.'

So when my mother packed my case she packed one for my naughty little sister as well, and my little sister helped her to fetch things for both the cases.

When my godmother-aunt was

ready to go, and I put my best hat and coat on, my sister said she must put *her* best hat and coat on too because she was going visiting just like her big sister.

Now you know there was a little gate that Mr Cocoa had made in the fence between his garden and ours, especially for my little sister so that she could come in to see Mrs Cocoa when she wanted to. It was a dear little gate and my little sister was always using it, but because she was going to visit Mrs Cocoa, she said she didn't want to go through her gate, she wanted to go through Mrs Cocoa's *front door.*

'I'm not Mrs Cocoa's next-door girl,' she said. 'I'm a visitor!'

So my father carried the case for her, and my little sister went down our front garden and through our front gate and through Mrs Cocoa's front

gate and *up* her front garden and Father lifted her up so she could knock on Mrs Cocoa's knocker.

My little sister knocked very hard and called out, 'Here I am, Mrs Cocoa; I've come to visit you!' And Mrs Cocoa opened the door, and said, 'Well, I *am* pleased to see you, come in do. You're just in time for tea.'

'Come in, my dear,' Mrs Cocoa said, and Mr Cocoa came out into the hall and said, 'I'll take your luggage, ma'am,' just as if he hardly knew my sister at all! Wasn't that nice?

My little sister said, 'Thank you, Mr Jones.' Not 'Mr Cocoa'. She said, 'Thank you, *Mr Jones*,' in a visitor-way.

Then she kissed our father 'good-bye' and Father said, 'Have a good time, old lady,' and then she was really on a visit by herself.

Mrs Cocoa gave my sister a very beautiful tea with all her best moss-rose tea-set on the table too, and that was exciting because although my sister had known Mrs Cocoa a long time she had never seen the moss-rose tea-set used before.

Then Mrs Cocoa took my sister upstairs to show her where she was going to sleep, and that was exciting too, because Mrs Cocoa had found a bed-cover with flowers and dragons and gold curly things needleworked all over it that my little sister had never seen before and this was on the little bed she was to sleep in.

There was a new picture on the wall too. Mrs Cocoa had told Mr Cocoa about the picture at my godmother-aunt's house, and kind Mr Cocoa had found a picture in a book and put it in a frame specially for the Visit. It was a picture of a singing lady lying in some water with flowers floating on it. Mr Cocoa said he liked the picture because the flowers and bushes and things in it looked so real.

My little sister liked the picture too. She said she liked it because the naughty lady hadn't taken her dress off, and she was wet as wet. She liked to have a picture of a naughty wet lady to look at, she said.

Weren't the Cocoas kind to think of all these nice surprises? Mr Cocoa said, 'We haven't got a piano, but I've got something else here that ought to keep you out of mischief.'

And do you know what he had? It was a musical-box! It was a little brown box with a glass window in the top, and at the side of the box there was a key. When you turned the key a little shiny thing with holes in it went round and round – you could see it through the glass window, and a pretty little tune came out of the box that Mr Cocoa said was called 'The Bluebells of Scotland'.

If you want to know what it sounded like perhaps you can ask someone to hum it for you.

Mr Cocoa showed my sister how to wind the musical-box and then he said she could play it whenever she liked. And she did play it – lots and lots of times while she was visiting.

My sister stayed with the dear Cocoa Joneses all that week-end and had a lovely time with them. She slept in the little bed and ate Mrs Cocoa's dinners and things and played the musical-box and went for walks with Mr Cocoa while Mrs Cocoa had a rest, and it was all very strange and pleasant.

But, do you know, my little sister NEVER ONCE CAME BACK HOME. She never even knocked on the wall to our mother! Not once. Mother said she saw my little sister playing in Mrs Cocoa's garden, and she watched her going off for walks, but my little sister didn't even look at our house!

She was really being away on a visit.

When the week-end was over, Mrs Cocoa packed her case for her, and Mr Cocoa took her home by the front door to show that she had been away.

When my little sister saw me again, she didn't ask about *my* visit – oh no!

She told me instead all about her visit to the Cocoas. She told me about the dragon and flower bed-cover and the naughty lady picture, and she said, 'There wasn't a piano, but I played another thing.'

My little sister couldn't remember the name of the musical-box though, so she said, 'I played a la-la box', and she la-la'd all the 'Bluebells of Scotland' tune for me without making one mistake. Wasn't she clever?

2. My Naughty Little Sister
and the guard

Do you like trains?

When I was a little girl I didn't like trains at all; but my little sister did. I thought that trains were horrid and noisy and puffy and steamy but my little sister said they were lovely things, and when she saw one she waved and waved and shouted and shouted to it.

Well now, one day a kind aunt wrote to our mother to ask if my little sister would like to go and stay for a week-end. All by herself.

Not with my father or mother, or

even with me, but all by herself like a grown-up lady!

My mother said, 'I don't think she's old enough,' and my father said, 'I don't think she's good enough,' and I said, 'She'll be too frightened.' Because, if you remember, she *had* been frightened about visiting people.

But my little sister said, 'I should like to go and stay for a week-end all by myself. I *am* an old enough girl, and I am not a frightened girl any more. I want to go!'

My mother didn't say anything and my father didn't say anything and I didn't say anything, and my little sister knew why that was, because she said, 'I'm not a good girl now, but I will be good as gold if you will let me go.'

So my father and mother said they thought she might go if she *was* as good as gold. So my little sister was good. She was quiet and tidy and whispery all the week and when the week-end came she *did* go away. All on her own.

This is the exciting thing that happened to her.

Our kind aunt lived quite a long way away, and my little sister had to go on a train *all by herself*.

Wasn't that exciting? All by herself. She had a little brown case with her nightdress inside, and her slippers and her dressing-gown and her best dress for Sunday and all the things she had taken to dear Mrs Cocoa's. My little sister carried Rosy-Primrose under her arm, but of course Mother carried the case to the station for her.

'Auntie will meet you at the other end,' Mother said. 'So she will carry it to her house for you.'

'I hope Auntie won't forget to look for me,' said my little sister, 'because I don't think I could open a train door all by myself.'

'That's all right,' our mother told her, 'I'm going to ask the guard to keep an eye on you.'

My little sister was going to say, 'What guard?' and ask questions and questions, but she knew that Mother was in a hurry to get the ticket.

When she got to the station she was very excited. She *wanted* to fidget and climb on all the parcels and run along the platform and peep at the man who puts the parcels on the weighing machine. But she didn't. She remembered about being good as gold. Wasn't she sensible?

When the train came in, she didn't

rush about or fuss, she walked nicely down the platform beside Mother to where the guard was standing, and when Mother stopped to speak to the guard my little sister didn't talk at all. She just stared at the guard because he was such a big beautiful man.

The guard had a big red beautiful face and a big fluffy black moustache and a golden glittery band on his cap and a silver glittery whistle round his neck and two beautiful flags – a red one and a green one under his arm. He gave my mother and my little sister a most pleasant smile.

'I am going to put this little girl in the end carriage, Guard,' our mother said, 'and I wonder if you would be kind enough to look after her ticket for her, and see that she gets off at the right station?'

The guard smiled very kindly then at my little sister. 'She is a very little girl,' he said. 'Is she a good child? If she is, she can come in the guard's van with me for the journey.'

My little sister thought she had

better say something, because she thought how nice it would be to travel in a real guard's van with a real guard, almost as nice as travelling with the engine-driver and not nearly so hot and coaly. She said, 'I am not always a good child. But I am being very good *this week*!'

So the guard said, 'That's good enough for me. In you go then,' and my sister climbed up into the guard's van.

He said, 'Sit on my little seat in the corner there.' And although it was rather a high little seat my little sister managed to climb on to it while the guard put her little case into the van, and picked up some parcels from the platform and put them in too.

Then the guard took his green flag, and blew his whistle, and Mother called out, 'Good-bye, give my love to Auntie,' and the train started to move. The guard jumped in quickly and shut the door. And they were off!

What a very nice man the guard was! He talked all the time to my little sister. He showed her a lantern that made red and green lights, and let her look at some sheets of paper with lines and printing on them that he said he had to write on every day. He lent my sister a pencil and let her scribble on the back of one of his pieces of paper, but it was very difficult because the train was so bumpy, so he gave her an apple to eat instead.

Each time the train stopped at a station the guard jumped down and took in parcels and sacks and put other parcels and sacks on to the platform. Sometimes there were railway porters waiting for the van, with trucks full of luggage, and they stared at my sister and asked the guard who she was. 'Oh, she's my new Mate,' the guard said, and my little sister felt proud as proud.

At one station the guard took in a big basket full of chickens, all looking out in a very pecky way. But the guard told my sister they wouldn't really hurt anyone. 'I often bring chickens,' he said, 'and ducks and dogs and cats.'

He said that one day he took a very growly dog that grumbled all the time. 'I was glad to see the back of him,' the guard said.

Then he said, 'Yes, I've looked after a lot of animals since I've been on the Line, but you are the first little girl.'

My little sister liked to think that

she was the first little girl to travel with the guard, and she said, 'If you have any other little girls to mind you'll be able to tell them about me.' And the guard said that he certainly would.

At last they came to the station that was near our aunt's house, and there was Auntie herself and two of our cousins as well, all waiting for her, and all so happy to see my little sister.

'There's Auntie!' my sister said, and she jumped up and down with excitement as the guard began to open the door.

But she remembered to be a polite child even though she was excited, and

before she went off she shook hands
with the guard and said, 'Thank you for
having me,' – just like a party – 'thank
you for having me.'

And the guard said, 'It has been
a real pleasure,' and when the train
moved off again, he stayed by his
window so as to wave to my little sister
and she waved to him. How our

cousins stared to see a guard waving from his guard's van window at my little sister.

So my little sister stayed with our auntie for a week-end and she wasn't naughty once. On Monday when she came back home Auntie came with her, because she wanted to come for the day to see our mother, so my sister didn't travel in the guard's van that time; but she remembered all about it, and when she and Bad Harry played trains in the garden she said, 'I must be the guard because I know all about it.'

And she did, didn't she?

3. Bad Harry and the milkman

Long ago, when my sister was a naughty little girl and not a grown-up lady, she had a friend called Harry. Harry was a naughty boy, so he and my sister were very good friends.

Harry and my sister were very noisy when they played together. If they saw anything funny they would laugh and laugh and roll about on the ground, and they always laughed at the same time at the same thing.

And when my sister was cross, Harry was cross, and when she was stubborn he was stubborn too, and when she said: '*I* want that!' about something, Harry always said: 'You can't have it, because *I* want it.'

My sister would shout, 'Give it to me at once!' and Harry would shout, 'No'.

Then my sister would jump up and down and say, 'Bad Harry' over and over again. 'Bad, bad, Harry!'

Then she would pull his hair, and he would pull her hair and they would hit each other in a very unkind way, until our mother came out and grumbled at them. Then they would stop fighting.

But they went on being friends just the same.

But when Harry came to our house or she went to Harry's house, she had to say 'Bad Harry' so many times that we called him Bad Harry in the end, and he really was, bad as bad. Oh dear.

They were cross good friends, weren't they?

Well now, when my sister and Harry were very small, they didn't come visiting each other on their own. Our mother took my sister to Harry's house, and Harry's mother brought him round to see us, and as our mothers were busy women they couldn't always be walking round to each other's houses, so there were some days when Harry and my sister couldn't see each other and they didn't like that at all.

One day, when it was cold and snowy, Harry's poor mother wasn't a very well lady, and she couldn't go out, so Harry had to stop at home and not see my sister, and he didn't like that.

Harry stood and looked out of the window, and saw the snow coming down, and everything looking very white and pretty, and he thought of all the lovely games he could have in the snow with my sister.

He thought of making snowballs and throwing them at her, as he'd seen the big boys making snowballs and throwing them at their friends, and he thought of them making a funny old snow-man with a pipe like a picture in one of his books. He thought of all sorts of nice games in the snow.

Then he got very cross and miserable in case the snow should melt before he could play with my sister again.

Then Harry had a bad idea (not a good idea – a *bad* one). He thought he would put on his coat and hat and go and visit my sister all on his own.

What a very bad Harry.

The next-door lady who had come in to make Harry's breakfast had gone home for a little while, and his mother was fast asleep in bed upstairs, so there was no one to ask.

Bad Harry went and fetched his coat and put it on. He wasn't good about buttons then, so he left it undone.

He found his woolly cap and he put

it on. He forgot his gloves, and his leggings and his shoes. He *was in such a hurry*.

He opened the front door, and off he went in his bunny-slippers down the path and out into the snow. He was excited; he hurried to get to our house to play with my sister.

The snow fell and fell. It was swirly and curly and cold and it blew into Harry's face, and it crunched under his bunny-slippers, and he thought it was very exciting.

Now all the people who lived in Harry's road had very kindly swept the snow from the pavements in front of their houses so it was quite easy for Harry to get along, but when he turned the first corner, he came to a road where the people hadn't been so kind and thoughtful about clearing the pavements, and soon his little bunny-slippers were quite covered up when he walked.

And his feet got wet and cold.

The wind was blowing down that street too, and it threw the snow into Harry's face in a very unkind way, and Harry suddenly found that his fingers were cold too.

His feet were cold and his fingers were cold, and he hadn't done his coat up so he was all cold. Cold as cold.

And because he was only a little boy then, Harry did a silly little boy thing. He stood quite still. He opened his mouth and he started to cry and cry.

Now, we had a very nice milkman who came to our house. He was a great friend of my little sister's. This milkman had an old white horse and a jingly cart and when he came down the road he would call out 'MILK-O! M-I-L-K-O!'

Like that, and when he came to the door he would sing, 'Milk for the babies, cream for the ladies! M-I-L-K-O!' He was a nice milkman.

He was *just* the person to come along with his white horse and jingly cart and find poor Bad Harry crying because he was cold.

Down the road he came, jingle jingle rather slowly because of the snow on the road, and his old white horse walking carefully, carefully. And he saw Harry.

He saw cold Harry crying so he said, 'Wo-a there,' to his old white horse, and the milk-cart stopped and he got down and said, 'Why, you're the little chap who plays with young Saucy down the next street.'

When the milkman said 'young

Saucy down the next street' he meant my sister because he always called her that (although it wasn't her name of course).

When the nice milkman saw how cold poor Harry was, and how miserable he was, he put him into his milk-cart and wrapped him up in a rug that was on the seat, and because he didn't know where Harry lived, he took him round to our house, which wasn't very far away – only round the next corner after all!

Now my sister was standing by *our* kitchen window being as cross as cross, and wanting to play in the snow with Harry, when she saw the milkman stopping at the gate.

She was very surprised when she saw him lift a bundle in a rug out of his cart and carry it up our path, so she ran to the door with Mother to see what it was all about.

When they opened the door they heard Harry bellowing and crying because he was so cold, and Mother thanked the milkman for bringing him and took him in quickly to warm by our fire.

Poor Harry! Mother rubbed and rubbed him and gave him hot milk and made him sit with his feet in a

bowl of hot water, until he stopped
crying and told her that he had come
round *all on his own.*

My sister *did* open her eyes when she heard this! On his own!

Mother told Harry that he had been *very naughty*. She said his mother might be very, very worried, and she sent me round at once to tell Harry's next-door lady where he was.

My sister stared hard at Harry when our mother told him he had been naughty and that his mother would be worried. When our mother scolded Harry he began to cry again, and this time my naughty little sister cried as well.

And they made so much noise that Mother forgave Harry and fetched him a biscuit, and he stopped crying.

My sister stopped crying too and Mother gave her a biscuit, and they sat quiet as quiet until I came back with Harry's shoes and some dry socks and leggings for him to put on, so that I could take him home again.

I told him that his next-door lady had said that his mother was still asleep and if we hurried we could get back before the poor not-well lady woke up.

So Harry hurried back with me and he was home again before his mother could wake up and worry.

Next day it was even more cold, and

when the milkman came my sister saw that he had put some funny little red-woollen bag things on his horse's ears.

She said, 'Why has your horse got those funny bag-things, milkman?'

And the nice milkman laughed and said, 'In case we have to pick up that bad friend of yours again. He yelled so much he made my horse's ears twitch. He might give her earache next time.'

And my sister looked very good, and she said in a very good quiet voice, 'I'm afraid Harry is a Bad Boy.'

4. The very old birthday party

Long ago, when my sister was a naughty little girl, we had a very old, old great-Auntie who lived in a big house with lots of other very old ladies and gentlemen.

Our mother used to go and visit this old Auntie sometimes and she used to tell us all about her. Then, one day our mother said, 'How would you like to come with me to visit Dear Old Auntie?'

Our mother said, 'She is going to have a birthday party next week, and

I think it would be very nice if you little girls could come to it. You see it is a very special party because old Auntie will be one hundred years old.'

One hundred years! That is very, very old. You ask some big person to tell you how old that means.

Well, *I* knew how old a hundred years was, so I said, 'Good gracious, what an old lady!'

My sister didn't know how old it was then because she was so little, but she said, 'Good gracious' too, because I had.

'She is a very sweet little old lady,' our mother told us. 'Everyone likes her.

The lady who looks after all the old ladies and gentlemen says that Dear Old Auntie is the *pride* of the Home.'

Wasn't that a nice thing for our old Auntie to be? The pride of the Home. We thought it was anyway, and we were very pleased to think that we were going to visit such a dear old lady on her one hundredth birthday.

Well now, when the birthday came, we were both very excited. We wore our best Sunday dresses and looked very smart girls.

Our mother had told us that we might take some money from our money-boxes to buy a present for our

Dear Old Auntie in the Woolworths shop. Our mother let us choose our own presents too. I bought our Dear Old Auntie a nice little white handkerchief with blue flowers on the corner. It took me a long time to think what to buy.

But my little sister didn't think at all. She knew just what she wanted. She said, 'I am going to buy one of those glassy-looking things with the little houses inside that make it snow when you shake them.'

My little sister had been to the Woolworths shop with Mrs Cocoa, so she knew all about these glassy things.

Do you know about them? They are very pretty.

I thought it was a silly thing to give to such a very old lady, but my naughty little sister said, 'It isn't silly. I would like one of those glassy things for *my* birthday!'

And she said she wouldn't buy anything else, so our mother took her along to the toy-counter and let her pay for one of the glassy things with her own money.

So, when we went to visit the Birthday Old Lady we had some nice presents for her. I had the handkerchief and my sister had the glassy thing with the snow inside it, and Mother had a box of sweeties from my father, and a nice woollen shawl that Mrs Cocoa Jones had kindly knitted from some wool that Mother had bought.

Wasn't she a lucky old lady?

My sister and I had never been to an old people's Home before, so we were very quiet and staring when we got there.

There were so many old people. Dear old ladies and dear old gentlemen all with white hair and smiling faces, and they all talked to us and waved to us and shook hands with us in a very friendly way.

And we smiled too. My sister smiled and smiled.

The lady who looked after the old people was called Miss Simmons and she was very kind.

'We are all very glad to see such young people,' she said to my sister. 'Do you know I don't think we've ever had anyone quite as young as you before?'

My sister was very pleased to think that she was the first very young visitor, and she did something that she sometimes did to Mr and Mrs

Cocoa Jones. *She blew kisses*. She was being nice.

Our Dear Old Great-Auntie was sitting by the fire in a big chair, and when Miss Simmons took us over to meet her, she was very pleased to see us.

What a very little old wrinkly pretty lady our old Auntie was! She had a tiny soft little voice and twinkly little eyes and she took a great fancy to my naughty sister at once. She asked her to sit next to her. Wasn't that a nice thing for my sister to be asked to do?

The old Auntie was very pleased with her presents. She put the shawl on straight away, and she put my handkerchief into her sleeve straight away too. But when she saw what my sister had brought she clapped her hands together in a funny old-lady way and she said, 'Well-well-well. What a lovely treat! I haven't seen one of these since I was a little girl. I saw one in another little girl's house and I always wanted one. Now I've got one at last!'

And the dear old lady shook up the glassy thing and made the snow fall on to the little house, and then she shook it again and made the snow fall again. She did it so many times that we knew how very pleased she was.

'Just fancy,' she said, 'I wanted one when I was a little girl like you, and I've got one today on my hundredth birthday.'

Miss Simmons said, 'I see you have a box of sweeties too. But I don't think you had better eat them yet. We have a birthday cake with one hundred candles for you to cut and a very nice birthday tea. It would be a pity to eat sweeties and spoil your appetite.'

Now my sister had heard Mother say that sort of thing to her but she was surprised to think that people had to say such things to old ladies, and she stared rather hard at her Dear Old Auntie.

And what do you think? When kind Miss Simmons went off to see about the birthday tea, old Auntie opened her box of sweeties, and gave one to me and one to my sister and then she ate one herself!

And she laughed and my sister laughed.

When Miss Simmons came back and saw what old Auntie had done she shook her finger at her. 'You are a very naughty old lady,' Miss Simmons said.

Then Miss Simmons looked at the

hundred-years-old lady, and my bad little sister, both laughing together and she said, 'Goodness me, you can see you are relations. *You both look alike*!'

And do you know, when I looked, and Mother looked, at the naughty old lady and my naughty little sister, we saw that they did!

5. The cross spotty child

One day, a long time ago, my naughty little sister wasn't at all a well girl. She was all burny and tickly and tired and sad and spotty and when our nice doctor came to see her he said, 'You've got measles, old lady.'

'You've got measles,' that nice doctor said, 'and you will have to stay in bed for a few days.'

When my sister heard that she had measles she began to cry, 'I don't want measles. Nasty measles,' and made herself burnier and ticklier and sadder than ever.

Have you had measles? Have you? If you have you will remember how nasty it is. I am sure that if you did have measles at any time you would be a very good child. You wouldn't fuss and fuss. But my sister did, I'm sorry to say.

She fidgeted and fidgeted and fussed and cried and had to be read to all the time, and wouldn't drink her orange-juice and lost her hanky in the bed until our mother said, 'Oh, dear, I don't want you to have measles, I'm sure.'

She was a cross spotty child.

When our mother had to go out to do her shopping, kind Mrs Cocoa Jones came in to sit with my sister. Mrs Cocoa brought her knitting with her, and sat by my sister's bed and knitted and knitted. Mrs Cocoa was a kind lady and when my little sister moaned and grumbled she said, 'There, there, duckie,' in a very kind way.

My little sister didn't like Mrs Cocoa saying, 'There, there, duckie,' to her, because she was feeling so cross herself, so she pulled the sheet over her face and said, 'Go away, Mrs Cocoa.'

But Mrs Cocoa didn't go away, she just went on knitting and knitting until

 my naughty
little sister
pulled
the sheet
down from her
face to see what Mrs
Cocoa could be doing and whether she
had made her cross.

But kind Mrs Cocoa wasn't cross –
she was just sorry to see my poor spotty
sister, and when she saw my sister
looking at her, she said, 'Now, I was
just thinking. I believe I have the very
thing to cheer you up.'

My sister was surprised when Mrs
Cocoa said this instead of being cross

with her for saying 'Go away,' so she listened hard and forgot to be miserable.

'When I was a little girl,' Mrs Cocoa said, 'my granny didn't like to see poor not-well children looking miserable so she made a get-better box that she used to lend to all her grandchildren when they were ill.'

Mrs Cocoa said, 'My granny kept this box on top of her dresser, and when she found anything that she thought might amuse a not-well child she would put it in her box.'

Mrs Cocoa said that it was a great treat to borrow the get-better box because although you knew some of the things that would be in it, there was always something fresh.

My little sister stopped being cross and moany while she listened to Mrs Cocoa, because she hadn't heard of a get-better box before.

She said, 'What things, Mrs Cocoa? What was in the box?'

'All kinds of things,' Mrs Cocoa said.

'Tell me! Tell me!' said my spotty little sister and she began to look cross because she wanted to know so much.

But Mrs Cocoa said, 'I won't tell you, for *you can see for yourself.*'

Mrs Cocoa said, 'I hadn't thought

about it until just this very minute; but do you know, I've got my granny's very own get-better box in my house and I had forgotten all about it! It's up in an old trunk in the spare bedroom. There are a lot of heavy boxes on top of the trunk, but if you are a good girl now, I will ask Mr Cocoa to get them down for me when he comes home from work. I will get the box out of the trunk and bring it for you to see tomorrow.'

Wasn't that a beautiful idea?

Mrs Cocoa Jones said, 'I haven't seen that box for years and years, it will be quite a treat to look in it again. I am sure it will be just the thing to lend to a cross little spotty girl with measles, don't you?'

And my naughty little sister thought it was just the thing indeed!

So, next morning, as soon as my sister had had some bread and milk and a spoonful of medicine, Mrs Cocoa came upstairs to see her, with her grandmother's get-better box under her arm.

There was a *smiling* spotty child waiting for her today.

It was a beautiful-looking box, because Mrs Cocoa's old grandmother had stuck beautiful pieces of wallpaper on the lid and on the sides of the box, and Mrs Cocoa said that the wallpaper on the front was some that had been in her granny's front bedroom, and that on the back had been in her parlour. The paper on the lid had come from her Aunty Kitty's sitting-room; the paper on one side had been in Mrs Cocoa's mother's kitchen, while the paper on the other side which was really lovely, with roses and green dickey-birds, had come from Mrs Cocoa's own bedroom wallpaper when she was a little girl!

My sister was so interested to hear this that she almost forgot about opening the box!

But she did open it, and she found so many things that I can only tell you about some of them.

On top of the box she found a lovely piece of shining stuff folded very tidily, and when she opened it out on her bed she saw that it was covered with round sparkly things that Mrs Cocoa said were called *spangles*. Mrs Cocoa said that it was part of a dress that a real fairy-queen had worn in a real pantomime. She said that a lady who had worked in a theatre had given it to her grandmother long, long ago.

Under the sparkly stuff were boxes and boxes. Tiny boxes with pretty pictures painted on the lids, and in every box a nice little interesting thing. A string of tiny beads, or a little-little dollie, or some shells. In one box was a very little paper fan, and in another there was a little laughing clown's face cut out of paper that Mrs Cocoa's granny had stuck there as a surprise.

My sister was so surprised that she smiled, and Mrs Cocoa told her that her granny had put that in to make a not-well child be surprised and smile. She said that she remembered smiling at that box when she was a little girl.

Mrs Cocoa's old granny had been very clever, hadn't she?

There were picture postcards in that not-well box, and pretty stones – some sparkly and some with holes in them. There was a small hard fir cone, and pieces of coloured glass that you could hold up before your eyes and look through. There was a silver pencil with a hole in the handle that you could look through too and see a magic picture.

There was a small book with pictures in it – oh, I can't remember what else!

It amused and *amused* my sister.

She took all the things out carefully and then she put them all back carefully. She shut the lid and looked at the wallpaper outside all over again.

Then she took the things out again, and looked at them again and played with them and was as interested as could be!

And Mrs Cocoa said, 'Well, I never! That's just what I did myself when I was a child!'

When my sister was better she gave the box back to Mrs Cocoa – just as Mrs Cocoa had given the box back to her granny.

Mrs Cocoa Jones laid all the things

from the box out in the sunshine in her back garden to air them after the measles. She said her grandmother always did that, and because Mrs Cocoa's granny had done it, it made it all very specially nice for my little sister to think about.

After that, my sister often played at making a get-better box with a boot-box that Mother gave her, and once she drew red chalk spots on poor Rosy-Primrose's face so that she could have measles and the get-better box to play with.

6. My Naughty Little Sister and the sweep

One morning, when I was a little girl and my naughty little sister was a girl littler than me, we went downstairs to breakfast and found everything looking very funny indeed.

The table was pushed right up against the wall, and the chairs were standing on the table and they were all covered over with a big sheet. The curtains were gone from the window, and the armchairs and the pictures and the clock and lots of other things. All gone!

My little sister was very interested to see all this, and when she looked out of the window, she saw that the armchairs and the pictures and all the other things were piled up in our back garden. My little sister did stare.

Clock and pictures and armchairs in the back garden, and things covered up with sheets, no curtains! Wasn't that a strange thing to find? My little sister said, 'We have got a funny home today.'

Then my mother told us that the chimney-sweep was coming to clean the chimney and that she had had to get the room ready for him. My naughty little sister was very excited because she had never seen a sweep, and she jumped and said 'Sweep,' and jumped and said 'Sweep,' again and again because she was so excited. Then she said, 'Won't we have any breakfast?'

'Won't we have any breakfast?' said my hungry little sister, because the chairs were standing on the table. And Mother said, 'As it is a lovely sunny morning you are going to have a picnic breakfast in the garden.'

Then my little sister was very pleased indeed because she had never had a picnic breakfast before.

She said, 'What shall we eat?' and my mother told her, 'Well, as it is a special picnic breakfast, I have made you some egg sandwiches.' Wasn't that nice? Sandwiches for breakfast! There was milk too, and bananas. My sister *did* like it!

We sat on the back doorstep and ate and ate and drank and drank because it was so nice to be eating our breakfast in the open air.

Then, just as my little sister finished her very last bite of banana, a big man with a black-dirty face came in the back gate and Mother said, 'Here is the sweep at last.'

Well, *you* know all about sweeps, but my little sister didn't, and she was so interested that my mother said she could watch the sweep so long as she didn't meddle in any way. My sister said she would be very good, so my mother found her one of my overalls, and tied a hanky round her head to keep her hair clean, and said, 'Now you can go and watch the sweep.'

My little sister watched the sweep man push the brush up the chimney and she watched when he screwed a cane on to the brush and a cane on to that cane, and a cane on to that cane, all the time pushing the brush up and

up the chimney, and she stayed as good
as good. She was very quiet. *She didn't
say a thing.*

She was so mousy-quiet that the
black sweep man said, 'You are quiet,
missy, haven't you got a tongue?'

My sister was very surprised when the sweep asked if she had got a tongue, so she stuck her tongue out quickly to show that she had got one, and he said, 'Fancy that now!'

Then my little sister laughed and the sweep laughed and she wasn't quiet any more. She talked and talked until he had finished his work.

Then my sister asked the sweep what he was going to do with all the soot he had collected and he said, 'I shall leave it for your father to use in his garden. It's good for frightening off the tiddly little slugs.'

So, when the sweep man went away

he left a little pile of soot in the garden for our father. My sister was sorry when he went away, and she asked my mother lots of questions. She wanted to know so many things that Mother said, 'If I answer you now I'll never get the place straight, so just you run off and play like a good girl, and I will tell you all about soot and chimney-sweeps later on.'

So my sister went off, and Mother cleaned up the room and brought in the chairs and hung up curtains and did all the other tidying up things and all the time my sister was very quiet.

There had been lots of things my

sister had wanted to know very badly. One thing she had wanted to know was if there was soot in *all* the chimneys. She wondered if there was any soot in her own bedroom chimney.

She went upstairs and looked up her chimney but she couldn't see because it was too dark up there.

It was very dark and my sister probably wouldn't have bothered any more about it, only she happened to remember that there was a long cane on the landing with a feather duster on the top, that Mother used for getting the cobwebs from the top of the stairs.

Yes, I thought you would guess.

The cane was very bendy and it wasn't difficult for a little girl to push it up the chimney.

Have you ever done anything so very silly as this? If you have you will know how dirty soot is. It's much dirtier than mud even.

My silly sister pushed the feather duster up her bedroom chimney and a lot of soot fell down into the fireplace. It was such a lot of soot and it looked so dirty that my little sister got frightened and wished that she hadn't done such an awful thing.

She couldn't help thinking that Mother would be very cross when she saw it.

So she thought she had better *hide it*.

You will never guess where that silly child tried to hide the soot. IN HER BED.

Yes, in her own nice clean little comfortable bed.

I'm glad to think that you wouldn't be so silly.

My sister made such a mess carrying the soot across the room and touching things with her sooty fingers and treading on the floor with sooty feet that she didn't know what to do.

She saw how messy her bedroom was and she was very, very sorry; she

was so sorry that she ran right
downstairs to the garden where
Mother was shaking the mats and she
flung her little sooty arms
round Mother's skirt,
and pushed her little
sooty face into Mother's
apron, and she said,
'Oh, I have been a bad
girl. I have been a bad
girl. Scold me a lot.
Scold me a lot.' And
then she cried and
cried and cried and
cried and
cried.

And she was so sorry and so ashamed that Mother forgave her even though it made her a lot of extra work on a very busy day.

My little sister was so sorry that she fetched things and carried things and told Mother when the sheets were dry and helped to lay the table for dinner and behaved like the best child in England, so that our father said it was almost worth having her behave so badly when she could show afterwards what a good girl she really was.

Our father was a very funny man.

7. My Naughty Little Sister
is very sorry

A long time ago, when I was a little girl with a naughty little sister, a cross lady lived in our road. This cross lady was called Mrs Lock and she didn't like children.

Mrs Lock didn't like children at all, and if she saw a boy or girl stopping by her front gate she would tap on her window to them and say, 'Don't hang about here,' in a very grumbling voice.

Wasn't that a cross thing to do? I will tell you why Mrs Lock was so cross. It was because she had a very beautiful garden outside her front door and once some boys had been playing football in the roadway, and the ball had bounced into her garden and broken down a beautiful rose-tree.

So when Mrs Lock saw children by her gate she thought they were going to start playing with footballs and damage her garden, and she always sent them away. Sometimes she came right out of the house and down to the gate and said, 'Go and play in the park – the roadway is no place for games,' and she would look so fierce and cross that the children would hurry away at once.

There was another reason too, why Mrs Lock was so cross. You see, she had a beautiful smoky-looking cat, and one day a nasty child had thrown a stone at the cat and hurt his poor leg, so if Mrs Lock saw a boy or girl stroking her smoky-looking cat, she would say, 'Don't you meddle with that cat, now!'

What a cross lady she was! But I suppose you couldn't really blame her. It isn't nice to have your rose-trees broken, and it's very, very bad to have your poor cat injured, isn't it?

Well now: one bright sunshiny morning, my naughty little sister went out for a little walk down the road all by herself. It was only a very small walk, just as far as the lamp-post at the corner of the road and back again, but my little sister was pretending that it was a very long walk; she was pretending that she was a shopping lady, stopping at all the hedges and gate-ways and saying that they were shops.

My little sister had a lovely game, all by herself, being a shopping-lady. It was a very nice day, and she had a little cane shopping-basket just like our mother's and a little old purse full of beads for pennies.

First my little sister stopped at a hedge and said, 'I'll have a nice cabbage today, please.' Then she picked a leaf and pretended that it was a cabbage, and put it carefully into her basket. She took two beads out of her purse and left them under the hedge to pay for it.

She went on until she came to a wall; there were two little round stones by the wall, so she pretended that they were eggs and bought them too.

Then she found a piece of red flower-pot which made nice meat for her pretend dinner. She had a lovely game.

Just as she arrived at Mrs Lock's

gate, the big smoky-looking cat jumped up on to it and began to purr and purr and as he purred his big feathery tail went all curly and twisty and he looked very beautiful. My sister stopped to look at him.

When the big smoky-looking cat saw my sister looking at him, he opened his mouth and showed her all his sharp little teeth, then he stretched out his curly pink tongue and began to lick one of his legs. He licked and licked.

My little sister was very pleased to see such a nice cat and she stood tippy-toed and touched him. When she did this he stopped licking and began

to purr again.

He was nice and warm and furry, so
she stroked him, very gently towards
his tail because Mother had told us
that pussies didn't like being stroked
the other way. 'Dear Pussy. Nice
animal,' she said to him.

Now, as my sister was such a little girl Mrs Lock didn't see her standing by the gate, so she didn't say 'go away' to her, and my sister had a long talk with the smoky-looking cat.

She told him that she was a shopping-lady. 'I have bought lots of things,' she said. 'I can't think of anything else.'

When she said this, the cat got up suddenly and jumped right off the gate back into Mrs Lock's garden, and as he jumped the gate opened wide. 'Meeow,' he said. 'Meeow' – like that.

My bad little sister looked through the gate and she saw the smoky cat going up the path. She saw all the pretty tulip flowers and the wallflowers growing on each side, and do you know what she said?

She said, 'That was very kind of you, Pussy. Now I can buy a nice cup to drink my milk out of.'

And she walked into Mrs Lock's garden. Mrs Lock's tulip flowers were all different colours: red, yellow, pink and white. You know that tulip flowers look rather like cups, don't you?

Yes. You know.

'I'll have a yellow cup, please,' my bad sister said. 'Here's the money, Pussy.'

And she picked a yellow tulip head and put it in her basket.

The smoky-looking cat walked round and round her legs, and his long tickly tail waved and waved and he said, 'Purr' to my little sister who was pretending to be a shopping-lady.

And Mrs Lock saw her from her front window.

Mrs Lock *was* cross. She tapped hard on her window glass and my naughty little sister saw her. Then she remembered that she wasn't really a shopping-lady, she remembered that she was a little girl. She remembered that it was naughty to pick flowers that didn't belong to you.

Of course you know what she did? Yes. She ran away, through the gate and down the road to our house, while Mrs Lock tapped and tapped and the smoky cat stood still in surprise.

My little sister ran straight indoors and straight upstairs and hid herself under the bed.

Mrs Lock came down the road after her, and when she saw my little sister run into the house, she came and knocked at our door, and told our mother all about my little sister's bad behaviour.

My mother was very sorry to hear

that my sister had picked one of Mrs Lock's tulips, and when Mrs Lock had gone, our mother went upstairs and peeped under the bed. You see, she knew *just* where her naughty little girl would be.

'Come out,' Mother said in a kind voice, because she knew my little sister was ashamed of herself, and my little

sister came out very slowly, and stood
by the side of the bed and looked very
sad; but Mother was so nice that my
sister told her all about the pretending
game and the pussy cat, and Mother
explained to her that you have to think
even when you're pretending hard, and
not do naughty things by mistake.

Then she told my sister all about

why Mrs Lock was cross. About her rose-tree and the nasty thing that had happened to the smoky-looking cat. And my sister was very, very sorry.

When Mother went downstairs again my sister had a good idea. She went to her toy-box and she found the beautiful card that our granny had sent her for her birthday. It had a pretty picture of a pussy cat and a bunch of roses on it. It was the nicest card my sister had ever had, but she thought she would give it to Mrs Lock to show that she was sorry.

She didn't say a word to anyone. She went out very quietly down the road to Mrs Lock's gate.

When she got there, my little sister went inside the gate and up the path. The smoky-looking cat came round the side of the house to meet her, but she didn't stop to stroke him. No. She went up to Mrs Lock's front door, and rattled the letter box, then she pushed the postcard inside. She put her mouth close to the letter box and shouted, 'I am sorry I took your flower, Mrs Lock. I am very-very sorry. I have brought you my best postcard for a present.' And then she ran away again. Only this time Mrs Lock didn't tap the glass.

The very next time my little sister

went by Mrs Lock's gate there was Mrs Lock herself, pulling weeds out of her pathway, and there was the smoky-looking cat sitting on a gatepost. When the cat saw my little sister he jumped down from the gatepost and said 'purr' to her and rubbed round and round her legs. Then Mrs Lock stood up very straight and looked over the gate at my little sister.

Mrs Lock said, 'Thank you for the card.'

All the time the smoky-coloured cat was purring and rubbing, rubbing and purring round and round my sister's legs and Mrs Lock said, 'My cat likes you. His name is Tibbles. Stroke him.'

And my sister did stroke him, and after that she stroked him every time she went past Mrs Lock's gate and found him sitting there in the sunshine. And although Mrs Lock often saw her stroking him she never said, 'Don't you meddle with my cat,' to her.

AND when Christmas-time came Mrs Lock sent my sister a card with robins and holly and shiny glittery stuff on it that was even more lovely than the pussy-cat card.

8. What a jealous child!

When my sister was a naughty little girl she had a godmother-auntie whom she loved very much.

This godmother-auntie was a very, very kind, and very, very pretty young lady. My little sister used to say that she was like a fairy in a book. She had curly gold hair and twinkling blue eyes and she was always laughing and singing.

And she was never cross. She used to have a lovely hat with cherries on it, and one day my greedy sister pulled the cherries off her hat and tried to eat them, and she didn't grumble at all. When she saw the dreadful face my naughty little sister was making when she found that those hat-cherries were full of nasty cotton-wool stuff she only laughed, and said, 'If you'd *told* me you wanted them to play with you could have had them, and then I would have explained that they were not real.'

And when our mother scolded my sister this pretty lady said, 'Don't worry, I was going to put a rose on that hat anyway.'

And the next time she came to see

us she *had* put a rose on her hat – a big pink one, and to please my little sister she had brought along a small pink rose for her to wear on *her* hat! 'Only don't try to eat that,' she said, 'because it is made of silk and won't taste at all nice.'

Wasn't she kind?

This beautiful godmother worked in a big sweet shop in London where they made specially grand sweets in a big kitchen behind the shop, and she used to tell my sister and me all about how the sweets were made.

She told us how the sweets were rolled in sugar and cut with real silver knives and how all the fruity pieces in them came right across the sea from France in wooden boxes, and we were very interested.

She always brought us a big box of sweeties from her shop and they were grander than any sweeties we'd ever seen before. They were in a very smart silky box with flowers on it, and the box was tied up with real hair-ribbony ribbon that our mother always put away in her ribbon box.

When our mother saw the beautiful tied-up box she always said, 'It looks too pretty to open.' But we *did* open it.

And when the box was opened she

would say, 'They look too nice to eat.'
But we *did* eat them, and Mother
always had the first one – and she
always took the almondy one in the
middle with the green bits sticking out
of it, because there was only one of
those, and she didn't want my sister
and me to be cross about who should
have it.

My little sister loved those boxes of

sweeties because her godmother-aunt had told her all about the big shop and the place where they were made, and she would be very careful before she chose her sweet, and when she did choose it she would say, 'Tell me about this one, Godma-aunt.'

And she would hear all over again about silver knives and French cherries and men in white caps who twisted the sweetie stuff on hooks and pulled it out and p-u-l-l-e-d it out to make it clear and shiny.

When her beautiful godmother said, 'Pulled it out' she would make pulling out faces and speak in a pulling out voice, she would say, 'P-u-l-l-e-d i-t o-u-t' – like that.

How my sister would laugh. She always wanted to hear about the pulling out of the sweetie stuff when her godmother came to see us.

We were always glad to see my little sister's godmother, she was so very nice. My little sister liked seeing her best of all. She liked to climb on to her godmother's lap and stare at her pretty smiley face. She would pat her cheeks and say, 'Sing to me, Godma-aunt. Sing me a funny song.'

And her godmother would sing her all sorts of funny songs until my sister's eyes got all peepy and teary with laughing so much.

Then my sister, who was not a kissing child at all, would hug and kiss her pretty godmother-auntie and say, 'I do love you, you nice lady!'

Wasn't she a lovely godmother to have?

Now, you wouldn't think that

anyone could ever be cross with such a dear lady, would you?

You would be surprised to hear that someone shouted at her and said, 'Go away, I don't want you,' wouldn't you?

I know I was surprised when my sister behaved like that to her dear godmother. But she did. And do you know why? It's because she was an unpleasant, jealous girl.

You see, one day her dear godmother brought a great tall man to see us. She had never brought anyone else before, and my sister didn't quite like it. She liked to have her godmother on her own. She said, 'I'm shy,' and

ran and hid her face in Mother's lap,
and when Mother told her to sit on
a chair and to stop being silly, she sat
and stared at her godmother-aunt and
the great tall man and looked cross
as cross.

Do you know why she behaved
like that?

It was because the great tall man
liked her godmother-aunt too and it
was because her godmother-aunt liked
the tall man very much.

My naughty little sister didn't want
her godmother to like anyone but her,
and she didn't want the big tall man to
like her godmother.

She was jealous. And that is a very nasty thing to be, isn't it? What a good thing you aren't a child like that.

My sister pretended that she didn't want any sweeties, and her poor godmother looked quite worried.

'But Albert made some of them,' she said.

Albert was the great tall man.

Our godmother started to tell us all about Albert making the sweeties, but my sister wouldn't listen. She got down from her chair and said, 'I want to go to bed now.'

Do you know that was in the morning, and she hadn't had her

dinner. Wasn't she being awkward?

Mother said, 'You behave yourself, you naughty little girl.'

But the beautiful godmother-auntie said, 'Don't be cross with her, I think she's not sure about Albert.'

She smiled very kindly at my sister and said, 'You must like Albert, duckie. Albert and I are going to get married very soon and we shall be living in a dear little house and you can come and stay with us.' And she came over to my sister in a kind way.

When my sister heard this, when she heard that the great tall man and her pretty godmother-aunt were going to be married, she was so cross that she said what I told you.

She said, 'GO AWAY. I DON'T WANT YOU.'

She said, 'I don't want you and I don't want that great tall man. You can go away now.'

Oh dear! Our mother was cross! But what do you think? That great big tall Albert man started to laugh, and he had such a loud roary laugh that my sister forgot to be jealous and stared at him.

When Albert laughed my sister's godmother began to laugh too, and they made so much noise that our mother began to laugh as well, and so did I – you never heard so much laughing.

Then that funny Albert man got up and opened a big bag that he had brought with him, and he took out a big, wide saucepan. Then he took out a bag of sugar and some butter and some treacle stuff in a tin. He was laughing all the time he did it because my sister was staring so much!

He took these things out to our mother's kitchen and he began to cook all the sugar and stuff in his saucepan. He didn't say anything, he just cooked.

No one had ever done a thing like that in our house before, so my sister went on being not jealous, and went out into the kitchen to see what he was doing instead.

When Albert saw my sister looking at him he put his hand into his bag and took out a white hat and *put it on his head.*

And he cooked and cooked and stirred with a spoon and cooked until all the sugar-butter-treacly stuff began to smell very nice indeed.

Then Albert took the saucepan off the stove, and did another funny thing.

He took the towel off the hook behind our kitchen door, and he wiped the hook very clean with our mother's dish-cloth and dried it beautifully on the tea towel.

My sister's eyes said 'O' 'O', she was so astonished.

Then, all of a sudden, Albert took the warm sticky stuff out of the saucepan and threw it over the hook.

Then he got a hold on the end of it and he p-u-l-l-e-d it and he p-u-l-l-e-d it. Then he twisted it up and he threw it back over the hook and he p-u-l-l-e-d and p-u-l-l-e-d it again, quick as quick.

It was just like my sister's godmother had told us. And it wasn't in the shop-kitchen either, it was in our own mother's own kitchen.

Albert pulled that stuff until it was clear and then he took it off the hook, quick as quick! It was all long and twisty.

It was a beautiful thing to do, wasn't it?

Albert didn't speak to my sister, he just spoke out loud to himself; he said, 'I wonder if it tastes all right?'

He got a hammer and began to

break the long twisty piece of toffee-stuff. When he did this, a piece jumped right off the table and fell by my sister's foot.

Our kitchen smelled so nice and the sweetie looked so nice, that my sister picked that piece up and popped it into her mouth and it was *quite delicious*.

Now she wasn't jealous at all. She was proud. She was proud to think that she knew such a clever man. 'It is very, very nice, Albert,' she said. 'You are very clever.'

Then she laughed and Albert laughed, and Albert let her put his funny white cap on, and her godmother lifted her up so that she could see herself in the glass wearing the white cap, and everyone was very happy.

My sister looked at her lovely smiling godmother and the great, tall, clever Albert and she said, 'I don't mind Albert being my godmother-uncle after all.'

9. The smart girl

One day, when I was a little girl and my little sister was sometimes naughty, the Mayor of our town invited us to a children's garden party. Bad Harry was invited too, and so were all the other children who lived near us.

When Mrs Cocoa heard that my little sister was going to the Mayor's party she was very pleased because she loved my bad little sister very much, and so she made her a beautiful party dress to wear.

Mrs Cocoa said that she had some nice material called Indian muslin in her drawer that would be just the thing for a party-dress.

The Indian muslin was all white with little white needlework flowers all over it. Mrs Cocoa made it into a dress for my little sister, and when it was finished she put a pink ribbon round the middle of it, and pink bows on the sleeves, and she made a frilly petticoat to go underneath it; and when my little sister tried it on she looked just like a beautiful new doll straight out of the box.

Bad Harry was there when my sister tried her dress on and he opened his eyes very wide.

'Nice,' said Bad Harry. 'You *do* look nice.'

And he said, 'Nice and nice and nice,' to show my sister how very smart he thought she looked.

My little sister didn't say anything. She just stood on the table and looked at herself in the mirror over the mantelpiece and was so very pleased she couldn't talk at all.

She was quite quiet until dear Mrs Cocoa said, 'Don't you like it?' Then she spoke. She said, 'Oh, Mrs Cocoa, I am just like a fairy. I think I must take it off quickly before it gets dirty.'

That was a surprising thing for my little sister to say, for as a rule she didn't mind being dirty a bit.

When our mother had taken the dress off for her, my funny sister ran to Mrs Cocoa and hugged her and kissed her and said, 'Dear Mrs Cocoa, I love my smart dress. I love it very much. *I love me in it, too.*'

She wouldn't hug Mrs Cocoa while she had the dress on, because she was afraid of spoiling it. Wasn't she funny?

Before the party day my little sister often went upstairs and asked our mother to let her peep into the wardrobe and see the Indian muslin dress, but she didn't want to try it on again, she wouldn't even touch it. She said she wanted it to be absolutely beautiful for the party. Wasn't she a strange child?

When the party day came, and she saw me getting ready to go, my little sister said, 'Mother, I will wear my smart dress *now*.' And she stood straight and good on a chair while Mother washed her, and straight and good when she was dressed, AND straight and good when her hair was brushed, because she wanted to look just like a fairy.

Bad Harry came to call for us. 'Come on, come on,' he said, because he was impatient, but my little sister would not hurry. She said, 'Good-bye' to our mother in a very quiet voice, and she took my hand like a good girl and walked along very neatly in her white shoes, not scuffling the dust or anything!

Mrs Cocoa came to her gate to see us off and my sister waved her hand to her. 'I can't kiss you, Mrs Cocoa,' she said, 'because I am all neat and nice,' and although Bad Harry said, 'Hurry! Hurry!' and ran ahead and back again and again she still walked very nicely and slowly with me.

At last we came to the Mayor's Garden Party place. It did look grand! The Mayor had hung lots of little coloured flags all round his garden, and the big gates were open and a

band was playing, and we could hear Punch-and-Judy noises and see stripy tents inside. Bad Harry was so excited that he just dashed ahead of us, and would have gone in on his own, if the gate man hadn't asked for his invitation card that I was carrying for him!

There were a lot of people crowding round the gate watching the children going to the party, and one lady said, 'Oh, the little duckie,' when she saw my neat and nice sister, and my little sister felt very proud. But she didn't turn her head, and she didn't let go of my hand, because she wanted to look as fairy-like as possible!

The Mayor had made a lovely party for us. We soon found that the stripy tents had all sorts of interesting things in them. Things that you could do without paying for them. It was just like a lovely *free* fair!

There were hoop-la's and magic fish-ponds and swings and pony-rides and Mr Punch and a conjurer, all as free as free. There was even a coconut shy, and we saw some of the bigger children throwing balls at the coconuts.

Wasn't it kind of the Mayor? We saw him walking in the garden with a gold chain round his neck, and he smiled at us and asked if we were having a good time. We said, 'Yes, thank you,' and he said, 'Good. Good.'

And we were enjoying ourselves. At least I was. And Bad Harry was. But my little sister didn't seem to be enjoying it very much at all. You see, she was afraid of spoiling her smart dress, and when the gentleman with the roundabouts said, 'Come on now, who wants a ride?' she couldn't say 'Me! Me!' because she wanted to look smart and she was afraid she might get her dress dirty on the roundabouts; and when the fish-pond young lady said, 'Come and fish for a magic prize,' she said, 'No, thank you, I might get wet!'

Bad Harry fished and he won a tin whistle, but, although she wanted a tin whistle very much, she wouldn't fish, oh no!

When we went to see Mr Punch she stood at the back of the crowd because of her sticking-out dress, and she was so far away that when Mr Punch smacked his baby, she didn't hear the nice man by the Punch show saying, 'It's all right, children, he isn't really hurting it, you know!' and so of course she cried, and then she had to stop crying because she might make her Indian muslin dress all teary.

Bad Harry got quite cross at last and he said, 'Why did you wear that silly old dress?'

My sister said, 'It's not silly. It's smart.'

And Harry said, 'It's smart *and* it's silly if you can't do anything in it.'

My little sister said, 'I want to be smart.'

Then Bad Harry said, 'Well, if you keep on being smart like that you won't be able to have any of the Mayor's nice tea that the ladies are putting on the tables in that big tent over there. It's a very nice tea,' Bad Harry said. 'There are lots of cakes and jellies. I know because I've just been over there to look.'

When my little sister heard about the tea and the jellies and when she thought about the roundabouts and the fish-pond she began to feel quite sorry. But she didn't want to spoil her smart dress.

She thought and thought. She saw the other children running about and sliding on slides and eating ice-cream and throwing balls at coconuts, and then she had a funny idea.

Very, very quietly she walked away

from the fair-place and round behind some bushes where no one could see her. I didn't notice her go, because Bad Harry and I were trying to throw rings over some hooks on the hoopla stall.

When I *did* find that she had gone, I was very worried, especially as a big gentleman in a red coat began to bang on a tray and call out, 'Now, children, line up, and we will go in to tea.'

I must say I didn't want to have to go and look for my sister just at tea-time. I thought that the other children might eat all the cakes and jellies and things before I found her, and I wouldn't like that much.

But I *had* promised to look after her, so I began to ask people if they had seen her.

I was just asking a lady, when I heard everyone burst out laughing.

All the boys and girls laughed, and the roundabout man, and the Punch man and the fish-pond lady, and the

Mayor and Bad Harry. They laughed and laughed and laughed.

They were laughing at my naughty little sister!

What do you think she had done?

She had got so tired of being careful of her beautiful dress that she had gone behind the bushes and *taken it off*. I don't know how she managed on her own – but she did.

She had taken off her dress and her lovely frilly petticoat and had put them very carefully over a garden seat, and out she jumped, her old noisy jumping self again, skipping up and down in her little white vest and her little white knickers! And she was laughing too.

'*Now* I can have swings, and fish-ponds, and roundabouts and a *big tea*,' she shouted. 'Now I can be ME again.'

She was very pleased with her good idea.

'I shan't spoil my beautiful dress now,' she said. 'Aren't I a clever girl?'

What would you have said if she had been your Naughty Little Sister?

10. My Naughty Little Sister
is a curly girl

There was a little girl called Winnie who used to come and see us sometimes when I was a little girl with a naughty little sister.

This girl Winnie was a very quiet, tidy child. She never rushed about and shouted or played dirty games, and she always wore neat clean dresses.

Winnie had some of those long round and round curls like chimney-pots that hung round her head in a very tidy way, and when Winnie moved her head these little curls jumped up and down. Mother told us that these curls were called *ringlets*.

One day, when Winnie and her mother were spending the afternoon at our house, my sister sat staring very hard at Winnie's ringlets, and all of a sudden she got up and went over to her and pushed one of her little fingers into one of Winnie's tidy ringlets.

Then, because the ringlet looked so nice on her finger, she pushed another finger into another ringlet.

Now, if anyone had interfered with *my sister's hair* she would have screamed and screamed – she even made a fuss when our mother brushed it – but Winnie sat still and quiet in a very mousy way, although I don't think she liked having her hair meddled with any more than my sister would have done.

Winnie's mother certainly didn't like it, and she said in a polite firm voice, 'Please don't fiddle with Winifred's hair, dear, the curls may come out.'

Then Winnie's mother said to our mother, 'They take such ages to put in every night.'

When Winnie's mother said this, my funny sister thought that the curls would come right out of Winnie's head if she touched them too much. And she thought that Winnie's mother would have to pick all the curls up and put them back into Winnie's head at night-time. So she stopped touching Winnie's hair at once, and went and sat down again.

She didn't think she would like to be Winnie with falling-out curls.

My little sister sat looking at Winnie though, in case a curl should fall out on its own, but when it didn't, she got tired of looking at her, and went out into the garden instead to talk over the fence to dear Mrs Cocoa Jones.

'Mrs Cocoa,' she said, 'Winnie has

funny curls.'

Mrs Cocoa was surprised when my sister said this, so she told her what Winnie's mother had said about the curls coming out.

Now, Mrs Cocoa was a kind polite lady and she didn't laugh at my little sister for making such a funny mistake. She just told her all about how Winnie's mother made Winnie's curls for her.

Mrs Cocoa told my sister how, when *she* was a little girl, her kind old grandmother had curled *her* hair. She said that her grandmother had made her hair damp with a wet brush and had twisted her hair up in little pieces of rag, and how she had gone to bed with her hair twisted up like this and how, next morning, when her grandmother had undone her curlers she had had ringlets just like Winnie's.

My sister was very interested to hear all this.

'Of course,' Mrs Cocoa said, 'my granny only did up my hair on Saturday nights so that it would be curly for Sunday. On ordinary weeknights I had two little pigtails like yours.'

When my sister heard Mrs Cocoa saying about how her grandmother curled her hair for her, she began to smile as big as that.

'I know, Mrs Cocoa,' she said, 'you can make me a curly girl.'

Mrs Cocoa said that my sister would have to sit still and not scream then, and my sister said she would be very still indeed, so Mrs Cocoa said, 'Well then, if your mother is willing, I'll pop in tonight and put some curlers in for you.'

After that, my sister went back into the house, and sat very quietly looking at Winnie and Winnie's beautiful ringlets and smiling in a pussy-cat pleased way to herself.

She didn't say anything to Winnie and her mother about what kind Mrs Cocoa was going to do, but when they had gone she told Mother and me all about it, and Mother said it was very kind of Mrs Cocoa to offer to make ringlets of my sister's hair, and she said, 'Mrs Cocoa can try anyway, although I can't think *how* you will sit still without making a fuss.'

But my sister said, 'I want ringlets like Winnie's,' and she said it in a very loud voice to show that she wouldn't fuss, so our mother didn't say anything else, and when Mrs Cocoa came over at my sister's bedtime, with a lot of strips of pink rag, and asked for my sister's hairbrush and a basin of water, our mother fetched them for her without saying a word about how my sister usually fussed.

Now, my sister had said that she wasn't going to be a naughty girl when Mrs Cocoa curled her hair, and she knew that Mother expected her to be naughty and that I expected her to be naughty, so, although she found that she didn't like having her hair twisted up into rags very much, *she was good as gold*.

My sister didn't like having her hair twisted up into those rags one bit. You

see, her hair was rather long, and Mrs
Cocoa had to twist *and* twist *very
tightly indeed* to make sure that the
curlers would stay in; and the tighter
the curl-rags were the more

uncomfortable they felt.

But my sister didn't say so. She sat very good and quiet and she thought about all those lovely Winnie-ringlets, and when Mrs Cocoa had finished she thanked her very nicely indeed and went upstairs with Rosy-Primrose, with her hair all curled up tight with little pink rags sticking up all over her head.

But, oh dear.

Have *you* ever tried to sleep with curlers in *your hair*? My sister tried and tried, but wherever she turned her head there was a little knob of hair to lie on and it was most uncomfortable.

She tried to go to sleep with her nose in the pillow but that was most feathery and unpleasant.

In the end the poor child went to sleep with her head right over the edge of the bed and her arm tight round the bedpost to keep herself from falling out.

That wasn't comfortable either, so

she woke up.

When my little sister woke up she shouted because she couldn't remember why she was lying in such a funny way, and our mother had to come in to her.

When Mother saw how hard it was for my little sister to sleep with her curlers in, she said perhaps they had better come out, and that made my naughty little sister cry because she did want Winnie-ringlets, until Mother said, 'Well, if you want curls don't fuss then,' and went back to her own bed.

After that my poor sister slept and woke up and slept and woke up all night, but she didn't shout any more, and when morning came she was sleepy and cross and peepy-eyed.

But when she had had her breakfast, Mrs Cocoa came in to undo the curlers, and my sister cheered up and began to smile.

She sat very still while kind Mrs Cocoa took out the rags and carefully combed each ringlet into shape, and when Mrs Cocoa had finished, and my sister climbed up to see herself in the mirror she smiled like anything.

And I smiled and Mother smiled.

She was a curly girl – curlier than Winnie even, because she had a lot more hair than Winnie had. She had real ringlets that you could push your fingers into!

My sister was a proud girl that day, she sat about in a still quiet way – just like Winnie did, and after dinner she fell fast asleep in her chair.

When my sister woke up she sat for a little while and did a lot of thinking, then she got down from her chair and went round to see Mrs Cocoa.

'Thank you very much, Mrs Cocoa, for making me a curly girl,' my sister said, 'but I don't think I will be curly any more. It makes me too sleepy to be curly.'

'I know why Winnie is so quiet now,' my sister said, 'it's because she can't sleep for curlers. I think I would rather be me, fast asleep with pigtails.'

And Mrs Cocoa said, 'That's a very good idea, I think. Anyway, who wants you to look like that Winnie?'

When My
Naughty
Little Sister
Was
Good

Contents

1. My Naughty Little Sister learns to talk

Once upon a time, when my sister and I were little children, we had a very nice next-door neighbour called Mrs Jones. Mrs Jones hadn't any children of her own, but she was very fond of my sister and me.

Mrs Jones especially liked my sister. Even when she was naughty! Even when she was a cross and noisy baby with a screamy red face, Mrs Jones would be kind and smiley to her, and say, 'There's a duckie, then,' to her.

And sometimes Mrs Jones would be

so kind and smiley that my bad little sister would forget to scream. She would stare at Mrs Jones instead, and when Mrs Jones said, 'Poor little thing, poor little thing,' to her, my sister would go all mousy quiet for her. My naughty little sister liked Mrs Jones.

When my sister was a very little baby girl, she couldn't talk at all at first. She just made funny, blowy, bubbly noises. But one day, without anyone telling her to, she said, 'Mum, Mum,' to our mother.

We were surprised. We told her she was a very clever baby. And because we were pleased she said, 'Mum,

Mum,' again. And again. She said it and said it and said it until we got very used to it indeed.

Then another day, when my sister was saying 'Mum, Mum,' and playing with her piggy toes, she saw our father looking at her, so she said, 'Dad, Dad,' instead!

Father was very excited, and so was Mother, because our funny baby was saying 'Mum, Mum,' and 'Dad, Dad,' as well. I was excited too, and so was dear Mrs Jones.

And because we were so excited my sister went on and on, saying 'Dad, Dad, Dad,' and 'Mum, Mum, Mum,' over and over again until Father, Mother and I weren't a bit excited any more. Only dear Mrs Jones went on being specially pleased about it. She was a nice lady!

So, one morning, when Mrs Jones looked over the fence and saw my baby sister in her pram, sucking her finger, she said, 'Don't suck your finger, ducky. Say, "Dad, Dad," and "Mum, Mum," for Mrs Jones.'

And what do you think? My funny sister took her finger out of her mouth and said 'Doanes'. She said it very loudly, 'DOANES' – like that – and Mrs Jones was so astonished she

dropped all her basket of wet washing.

'Doanes, Doanes, Doanes,' my sister said, because she couldn't quite say 'Jones', and Mrs Jones was so pleased, she left all her wet washing on the path, and ran in to fetch Mr Jones to come and hear.

Mr Jones who had been hammering

nails in the kitchen, came out with a hammer in his hand and a nail in his mouth, running as fast as he could to hear my sister say 'Doanes'.

When she said it to him too, Mr Jones said my sister was a 'little knock-out', which meant she was very clever indeed.

After that my sister became their very special friend.

When she got bigger she started to say other words too, but Mr and Mrs Jones still liked it best when she said 'Doanes' to them. If she was in our garden and they were in their garden they always talked to her. Even when she could walk and get into mischief they *still* liked her.

One day a very funny thing happened. Mrs Jones was in her kitchen washing a lettuce for Mr Jones's dinner when she heard a little voice say 'Doanes' and there was my naughty little sister standing on Mrs Jones's back door-step. AND NO ONE WAS WITH HER.

And my little sister was smiling in a very pleased way.

The back gate was closed and the side gate was closed, and the fence was so high she *couldn't* have got over it.

Mrs Jones was very pleased to see

my sister, and gave her a big, big kiss and a jam tart; but she was surprised as well, and said, 'How did you get here, duckie?'

But my little sister still didn't know enough words to tell about things. She just ate her jam tart, then she gave Mrs Jones a big kiss-with-jam-on, but she didn't say anything.

So Mrs Jones took my sister back to our house, and Mrs Jones and Mother wondered and wondered.

The very next day, when Mrs Jones was upstairs making her bed, she heard the little voice downstairs saying, 'Doanes, Doanes!', and there was my sister again!

And the back gate was shut, and the side gate was shut, and the fence was still too high for her to climb over.

Mrs Jones ran straight downstairs, and picked my sister up, and took her home again.

When Mr Jones came home, Mrs Jones told him, and Mother told Father, and they all stood in the gardens and talked. And my sister laughed but she didn't say anything.

Then I remembered something I'd found out when I was only as big as my sister was then. Right up by a big bush at the back of our garden was a place in the fence where the wood wasn't nailed any more, and if you were little enough you could push the wood to the side and get through.

When I showed them the place, everybody laughed. My sister laughed very loud indeed, and then she went through the hole straight away to show how easy it was!

After that, my sister was always going in to see Mrs Jones, but because the hole was so small, and my sister was growing bigger all the time, Mr Jones found another place in his fence, and he made a little gate there.

It was a dear little white gate, with

an easy up and down handle. There was a step up to it, and a step down from it. Mr Jones planted a pink rose to go over the top of it, and made a path from the gate to his garden path.

All for my sister. It was her very own gate.

And when Mrs Jones knocked on

our wall at eleven o'clock every morning, and my sister went in to have a cup of cocoa with her, she didn't have to go through a hole in the fence, she went through her very own COCOA JONES'S GATE.

2. My Naughty Little Sister's toys

Long ago, when my sister and I were little girls, we had a kind cousin called George who used to like making things with wood.

He made trays and boxes, and things with holes in to hang on the wall for pipes, and when he had made them he gave them away as presents.

George made me a chair for my Teddy-bear and a nice little bookcase for my story-books. Then George thought he would like to make something for my little sister.

Now that wasn't at all easy, because my sister was still a very little child. She still went out in a pram sometimes, she could walk a bit, but when she was in a great hurry she liked crawling better. She could say words though.

My sister had a very smart red pram. She liked her pram very much. She was always pleased when our mother took her out in it. She learned to say, 'pram, pram, pram,' when she saw it, and 'ride, ride, ride,' to show that she wanted to go out.

Well now, kind Cousin George was sorry to think that my sister liked crawling better than walking, so he said, 'I know, I will make her a little wooden horse-on-wheels so she can push herself along with it.'

And that is just what he did. He made a strong little wooden horse, with a long wavy tail, and a smiley-tooth face that he painted himself. He painted the horse white with black spots. Then he put strong red wheels on it, and a strong red handle. It was a lovely pushing-horse.

I said, 'Oh, isn't it lovely?' and I pushed it up and down to show my sister. 'Look, baby, gee-gee,' I said.

My sister laughed. She was so glad

to have the wooden horse. She stood up on her fat little legs and she got hold of the strong red handle, and she pushed too!

And when the horse ran away on his red wheels, my sister walked after him holding on to the red handle, and she walked, and WALKED. Clever Cousin George.

Mother said, 'That's a horse, dear. Say "Thank you, Cousin George, for the nice horse",' and she lifted my sister up so that she could give him a nice 'thank you' hug, because of course that was the way my sister thanked people in those days.

Then Mother said, 'Horse, horse, horse,' so that my sister could learn the new word, and she patted the wooden horse when she said it.

But my sister didn't say 'Horse' at all. *She* patted the wooden horse too, but she said, 'Pram, pram, pram.'

And she picked up her tiny Teddy-bear, and she laid him on the pushing-horse's back, and she picked up my doll's cot blanket and covered Teddy up with it, and she pushed the horse up and down, and said, 'Pram.'

When George came to see us again, he was surprised to find that my funny little sister had made the horse into a

pram, but he said, 'Well, anyway, she can walk now!' And so she could. She had stopped crawling.

Because George liked my little sister he made her another nice thing.

He made her a pretty little doll's house, just big enough for her to play with. It had a room upstairs, and a room downstairs, and there were some pretty little chairs and a table and a bed in it that he had made himself.

When my sister saw this doll's house she smiled and smiled. When she opened the front of the doll's house and saw the things inside she smiled a lot more.

She took all the chairs and things out of the doll's house and laid them on the floor, and she began to play with it at once. But she didn't play houses with it at all.

Because there was a room upstairs
and a room downstairs and a front that
opened she said it was an oven!

She pretended to light a light inside
it, just as she had seen our mother do,

when she was cooking the dinner, and she said, 'ov-en, ov-en.'

She called the chairs and table and the bed 'Dinner', and she put them back into the doll's house again, and pretended they were cooking, while she took tiny Teddy for a ride on the pushing-horse pram.

She played and played with her doll's house oven and her pushing-horse pram.

Our Cousin George said, 'What an extraordinary child you are.' Then he laughed. 'That gives me an idea!' he said.

And when he went away he was

smiling to himself.

The next time George came he was still smiling, and when my sister saw what he had made she smiled too. This time she knew what it was.

George had made a lovely wooden pretending-stove with two ovens and a pretending fire, and a real tin chimney. We don't have stoves like these nowadays, but some people still did when I was young. There was one in our granny's house.

My sister said, 'Gran-gran oven,' at once.

I gave my little sister a toy saucepan and kettle from my toy box, and

Mother gave her two little patty-tins.

George said, 'You can cook on the top, and in the ovens – just like Granny does.'

And that was just what my sister did do. She cooked pretending dinners on the wooden stove all day long, and Cousin George was very pleased to think she was playing in the right way with something he had made for her.

But that isn't the end of the story. Oh no.

One day my naughty little sister's bad friend Harry came to visit us with his mother. He was only a little baby boy then, but he liked playing with my sister even in those days.

When my little sister saw Harry, she said, 'Boy-boy. Play oven.' She wanted Harry to cook dinners too.

Bad Harry looked at the wooden stove, and the real tin chimney and the pretending fire, and he said, 'Engine. Puff-puff.'

Then Harry pretended to put coal into the little fireplace. He opened the oven doors and banged them shut again just like the man who helped the engine-driver did, and he made choof-choof-choofy train noises.

Harry had been with his father to see the trains and he knew just the

right noises to make and the right
things to do.

My sister didn't know anything about trains then, but it was such a lovely game that she made all the noises Harry made and said 'Engine' too.

After that she and Harry had lots of lovely games playing engines with the little wooden stove.

When Cousin George heard about this, he said, 'Pram-horses and oven-doll's houses, and now – engine-stoves!'

He said, 'It's no good. When that child is a bigger girl I shall just give her some wood and some nails and let her make her own toys!'

I think he must have forgotten that

he said this, because he never did give her any wood and nails. I wonder what she would have made if he had?

3. My Naughty Little Sister
and the twins

When my sister was still quite a little child, she liked looking at herself in the looking-glass. She was always asking someone to lift her up so that she could see herself.

She would stare and stare at her funny little self. She made funny faces, and then she would laugh at the funny faces she had made, and then laugh all over again because the little girl in the glass was laughing. She used to amuse herself very much.

When my sister had first seen

herself in the mirror she hadn't liked it at all. At first she had been pleased to see the small baby-girl, and had smiled, but when the baby in the glass smiled back, and she put out her hand to touch that baby-girl's smiley face – there had only been cold, hard glass. It had been so nasty and so frightening that my poor little sister had cried and cried.

Mother hushed and hushed her and walked up and down with her, and said, 'Don't cry! Don't cry! It's only you, baby, it's you in the glass.'

When my sister stopped crying, my mother lifted her up again, and said,

'It's you, baby, in the glass.'

And my sister looked at the poor teary baby in the glass, and she saw that the baby was copying her. She touched the glass again, and the baby touched it too. She got so interested she wasn't frightened any more. She said, 'Baby-in-the-glass!'

So after that, whenever my sister looked at herself in a looking-glass she said, 'Me. Me baby-in-glass.'

When she was neat and nice in a pretty new dress, she said, 'Smart baby-in-glass.' When she saw a dirty little face looking at her she said, 'Dirty baby-in-glass.'

She was a very funny child.

One day we went with our mother to fetch Father's shirts from the Washing Lady's house. Mother did most of our washing, but she sent Father's best shirts to the Washing Lady's house, because she washed them so beautifully and ironed them so cleverly they always looked like new.

Our Washing Lady had a funny little house. Inside her front door there was a room with pictures of ships on the wall, and photographs of sailors on the mantelpiece and seashells on the table.

The sailors were our Washing Lady's sons, and the ships were the ones they sailed the seas in. The Washing Lady was always talking about them.

There was always a steamy smell in the Washing Lady's house, because she was always boiling washing, and an ironing smell because she was always ironing things while the washing was boiling, and there was often a baking smell too, for this kind lady made beautiful curranty biscuits to give to the children who came with their mothers to fetch the washing.

My sister loved to go to the Washing Lady's house.

On the day I'm telling you about, a very funny thing happened when we got to the Washing Lady's house. We knocked at the door as we always did, and then we opened the door as we always did.

Out came a steamy smell and an ironing smell and a baking smell, just as they always did, too.

And then Mother called out, 'May I come in?'

And instead of the Washing Lady standing among the ship and sailor pictures and the seashells, we found two little tiny girls, standing hand in hand; and when they saw our mother and my little sister and me, they opened their mouths and they both called, 'Grandma, Grandma!'

My little sister stared and stared and stared. She looked at those little girls so much that they both stopped calling and stared back at her.

My sister stared so hard because those tiny little girls were absolutely alike. They had the same little tipping-up noses, the same little twinkly eyes, the same black, curly hair with red ribbons on, the same little blue dresses, the same red socks. *And they had both said 'Grandma' in the same little voices.*

Then the Washing Lady came out from the back room, and the two little alike girls ran to her, and hung on to her apron.

Mother said, 'These must be your Albert's twinnies then?'

And the Washing Lady said, 'Yes, they are.'

Albert was the Washing Lady's youngest sailor-son. She told Mother that the little girls had come to spend the day with her. She said, 'Albert's boat has come in, and their mother has gone to London to meet him.'

When she said this, the little looking-alike girls smiled again. They said, 'Our daddy is coming home!'

One twinnie said, 'From over the sea –' The other twinnie said, 'In a big, big boat –'

And the first twinnie said, 'And he's going to bring us –' And the other one said, 'Lots and lots –'

And they both said together, 'Of

lovely presents. HOORAY!'

And the funny twinnies fell right down on the floor and kicked their legs in the air to show how happy they were and they laughed and laughed.

My little sister thought they were so funny that she laughed and laughed too, and she fell on the floor and kicked *her* legs in the air. We all laughed then.

Then the Washing Lady told the twinnies to go and fetch the biscuit tin, and they went and fetched it. She gave me a curranty biscuit, and then one to my sister, then she gave one to each of the little twinnies. Then my little sister and the looking-alike girls sat down on the Washing Lady's front step to eat the biscuits, while their grandma packed up Father's shirts.

When my little sister finished eating her biscuit, she looked very hard at the twins. First at one twin, then at the other twin. Then she put out her hand and touched one little twinny face, and then the other twinny face. She was very quiet, and then she said, 'Which is the looking-glass one?'

That silly little girl thought one twinnie was a real child, and one was a looking-glass child. That was why she touched their faces, and when she couldn't feel any cold, hard glass she was very, very puzzled.

'Which is the looking-glass baby?' she said.

'Good gracious me, what will you ask next?' said our mother. Then she remembered how my sister liked looking at herself in the glass. 'Why,' she said, 'she thinks only one of them is real!'

Our Washing Lady laughed, but she was a kind lady. She said, 'They are twinnies, dear. Two little girls. There are two looking-glass babies just like them.'

And although she was a very busy

lady, she took my little sister and the twinnies upstairs to her bedroom, and showed my sister herself and *two* little looking-alike girls in the wardrobe mirror.

My sister looked at herself in the glass. She looked at the twinnies in the glass. Then she said, 'Thank you very much,' in a funny little voice.

And when we walked home she whispered to me, 'Is there another little real girl like me somewhere?'

I said, 'Oh no, there couldn't be anyone else like you – not anywhere.'

4. The six little Hollidays

Usually, when my sister and I were children, if our mother had to go anywhere special she would take my naughty little sister with her. But if it was somewhere very special indeed she left my sister with Mrs Cocoa Jones next door, or with Bad Harry's mother. Once my sister even spent a day at school with me.

But there was a time once, when Mrs Cocoa was away, and Bad Harry's mother was ill, when my mother didn't quite know what to do about getting my little sister minded.

Mother asked my teacher if my little sister could come to school again, but Teacher said that although she had been such a good child, she wouldn't be able to have her any more because she had minded some other little sisters in the school who hadn't been good at all. They had been so fidgety and naughty that she had had to say, no more minding!

The teacher said, 'I am afraid they are not all good like your little girl.'

Just fancy that!

Well, my mother was very anxious about my sister, because she knew my sister could be very shy with people. She couldn't think of anyone who might want to mind a shy, cross girl for a whole afternoon.

When she was coming back from the school, she met a lady she knew and told her all about it. The lady was called Mrs Holliday, and Mrs Holliday said at once, 'Oh, don't worry about that. We will mind her with pleasure. We will call round for her at two o'clock.'

My mother was very glad that Mrs Holliday was going to mind my sister, although she couldn't help wondering if my sister would behave herself.

When our mother told my sister that she was going to spend an afternoon with Mrs Holliday my sister looked very cross and frightened. She stuck her lip out and her face went red as red, and our mother said, 'Oh dear, don't be awkward, will you?'

I think my sister *would* have been awkward. She might have bellowed and shouted, but just then there was a knock on our back door and there stood Mrs Holliday herself, all ready and smiling, and behind Mrs Holliday, looking as shy and peepy as my little sister herself, were five little children: three little boys and two little girls.

Right up at the end of our garden by the back gate stood a very tall, very wide sort of perambulator-pushchair, and peeping out from under the hood of that was another little child!

My sister *did* stare, and all the little Hollidays stared. Mrs Holliday was a lady with red, rosy cheeks, and all the children had red, rosy cheeks too. And although they all wore different coloured coats and scarves they all wore bright blue woolly hats.

'We won't come in,' Mrs Holliday said, 'because our shoes are muddy.'

When my sister was ready, Mrs Holliday said, 'Come along, dear, don't take any notice of my children. They are all *very shy*, but they will talk nineteen to the dozen as soon as they are used to you.'

My sister was a shy child, but she had never seen so many shy children together before, and she quite forgot her own shyness when she saw them all hiding behind their mother.

Our mother said she hoped Mrs Holliday wouldn't find my sister too much for her, but Mrs Holliday said, 'One more will hardly be noticed.'

Then Mrs Holliday called the children out from behind her and said, 'These boys are John and David, and they are twins. This is Jean, and this is Susan, and they are twins too. The big boy Tom, he has a bad arm, so he is not at school today, and the baby is Billy.'

Then Mrs Holliday told Jean and Susan to take my little sister's hands, and off they all went, all shy and quiet and peepy, down the garden to the back gate and the big perambulator-pushchair.

There sat baby Billy with his legs dangling down under a shiny black cover like a pram cover. He was peeping out from under a big black hood like a pram hood. There was a handle behind the hood like a pushchair handle.

My sister was so surprised to see this funny pram-pushchair, she said, 'That's a funny thing.'

When my sister said this, all the little Hollidays laughed together, and stopped being shy, because they thought it was a funny thing too, and then they waited for their mother to tell my little sister all about it.

Mrs Holliday said, 'It's a very special chair, this is. It was once used by FOREIGN ROYALTY.' And she looked so pleased and so proud when

she said this, that my sister knew it must be something very grand.

Mrs Holliday said, 'It was specially made for Royal Twins – that is why it is so wide; and although it's nearly fifty years old, it's still as good as new.'

Mrs Holliday said that as my sister was a visitor, she could ride with Billy in the royal pushchair, and my sister was so pleased she could hardly remember to say 'good-bye' to our mother.

Off they went down the street, Mrs Holliday behind the perambulator-pushchair with little Hollidays on either side, and my little sister very smiling and pleased and not shy, with

Billy beside her. Billy was a dear little baby boy, and when he saw my sister was smiling and pleased, he was smiling and pleased too. They looked very happy children.

As they went along everybody they met smiled to see the funny pram-pushchair and the rosy Hollidays with their blue woolly hats and my happy little sister.

Mrs Holliday took them through the park, and they went a way my sister hadn't been before, so it was very interesting. In the park my sister got out of the pram-pushchair and ran and scuffled in the leaves with the other children. The leaves lay all over the paths, red and yellow and brown, and all the little Hollidays shouted with excitement and my sister shouted too.

When Mrs Holliday thought they had played enough they went off again. This time one of the little girl twins rode with Billy, and my little sister ran through the park with the other children. It was fun!

Outside the park, Tom, who had the bad arm, said, 'Before we go home we are going to the baker's, aren't we, Mother?'

And all the other little Hollidays shouted, 'Yes. Yes. For cookie-boys.'

They were all very excited, so my sister got excited too and they went down a street and stopped outside a funny little baker's shop.

Mrs Holliday said that as my sister hadn't been there before she could come in with her. All the Holliday children stood outside and pushed their faces against the window to watch.

Inside the shop was a dear old lady,

and when she saw Mrs Holliday she said, 'I know what you have come for: six cookie-boys.'

But Mrs Holliday said, 'Not six. *Seven* today. I've got an extra little child, who has never had one of your cookie-boys before.'

The old lady said, 'Then I must find her a very nice one.'

She took down a big wooden tray, and in it there lay dozens and dozens of shiny brown cookie-boys.

Do you know what cookie-boys are? They are buns made in the shape of funny little men, with currant eyes and noses and mouths and rows of currants all down their fronts for buttons!

The old lady's cookie-boys were the shiniest and the stickiest cookie-boys ever made, and people came a long way to buy them.

The old lady put six cookie-boys in a bag for Mrs Holliday, and then she chose a special one and put it in a special bag for my little sister.

When they got to Mrs Holliday's house, they all sat round a big table and had tea and bread-and-butter and jam, and when they had eaten and eaten, they finished off with their cookie-boys.

My sister had just finished eating hers when our mother came to fetch her.

And what do you think? When she saw my mother, my sister began to cry and cry. She said, 'I don't want to go home yet.'

Our mother was very surprised.

But Mrs Holliday said, 'Now, be a good girl, and you shall come another day.'

And my sister stopped crying at once. And she did visit them again, too.

5. The bonfire pudding

When my sister was a little girl she didn't like Bonfire Night and fireworks. She didn't like them at all. I liked them very much and so did my sister's friend Harry, but she didn't.

She wouldn't even look out of the window on Bonfire Night.

She would say, 'It's burny and bangy, and I don't like it.'

So on Bonfire Nights, Mother stayed home with her, while our father took me out to let the fireworks off.

It was a pity because our mother

did like fireworks.

Well now, one day, just before the Fifth of November (which is what Bonfire Night day is called) our mother took us round to our grandmother's house to pay a visit, and Mother told Grannie all about my little sister not liking fireworks.

She said, 'It's such a pity, because this year the fireworks are going to be very grand. There is going to be a big bonfire on the common, and everyone is going there to let off fireworks.'

She said, 'There is going to be a Grand Opening with the Mayor, and a Band on a Lorry.'

Our mother said, 'I am sure she would like it. She likes music.'

But my sister looked very cross. She said, 'I do like music very much. But I don't like fireworks.'

Mother said, 'But they are going to have baked potatoes and sausages and spicy cakes and all sorts of nice things to eat.'

My sister said, 'I don't like bonfires.'

Mother said, 'You see, she is a stubborn child. She won't try to like them.'

But our grannie wasn't a bit surprised. She said, 'Well, I don't like bonfires or fireworks either. I never did.

I was always glad to get my children out of the house on the Fifth of November. It gave me a chance to do something much more interesting.'

My little sister was glad to know that our grandmother didn't like fireworks either, so she went right up to Grannie's chair and held her hand.

Grannie said, 'You don't like fireworks and no more do I. Why don't you come and visit me on Firework Night? I think I can find something interesting for you to do.'

When Grannie said this, she shut one of her eyes up, and made a funny face at my sister. She said, 'Why don't you come and have some fun with me? Then your mother can go to the common with your daddy and sister and have fun too.'

My sister made a funny face back at Grannie, and said, 'Yes, I think I should like that.'

So on Bonfire Night, before it got too dark, Mother wrapped my little sister up in a warm coat and a big shawl and put her in a pushchair and hurried round to Grandmother's house.

She left my sister as soon as Grannie opened the door, because she was in a hurry to get back.

'Come in,' said Grannie to my little sister. 'You are just in time.' She helped my sister take her things off, and then she said, 'Now, into the kitchen, Missy.'

It was lovely and warm in the kitchen in our grannie's house. My sister was very pleased to see the big fire and the black pussy asleep in front of it.

'Look,' said Grannie. 'It's all ready.'

Grannie's big kitchen table looked just like a shop, there were so many things on it. There were jars and bottles and packets, full of currants and sultanas and raisins and ginger and candied peel and a big heap of suet on a board, and a big heap of brown sugar on a plate. There were apples and oranges and lemons, and even some big clean carrots!

There was a big brown bowl standing on a chair that had a big, big, wooden spoon in it. And on the draining board were lots of white basins.

Can you guess? My sister couldn't. She didn't know what all this stuff was for, so Grannie said, 'We are going to make the Family Christmas Puddings.

I always make one for every one of my children every year. And I always make them on Bonfire Night. IT TAKES MY MIND OFF THE BANGS.'

My sister was very surprised to hear this, and to know that all these lovely things to eat were going to be made into Christmas puddings.

Grannie said, 'You can help me, and it will take your mind off the bangs, too.'

She said, 'I've looked out a little apron; it will just fit you. It used to belong to one of your aunties when she was a little girl.'

And she tied a nice white apron

round my sister's little middle.

'Now,' Grannie said, 'climb up to the sink, and wash and scrub your hands. They must be clean for cookery.'

So my sister climbed up to the sink and washed her hands, and Grannie dried them for her, and then she was ready to help.

Grannie found lots of things for her to do, and they laughed all the time.

Grannie was quick as quick, and every time my sister finished doing one thing, she found something else for her to do at once.

Grannie poured all the currants out on to the table and my sister looked to see if there were any stalky bits left in them. When she had done that, Grannie told her to take the almonds out of the water, and pop them out of their brown skins. That was a lovely thing to do. When my sister popped an almond into her mouth Grannie only laughed and said, 'I'll have one as well.'

Grannie chopped the suet, then the almonds, and the ginger while my sister put the currants and sultanas and things into the big brown bowl for her. It was quite a hard job because she had to climb up and down so much, but she did it, and she didn't spill anything either. Grannie was pleased.

Grandmother chopped the candied peel, and because my sister was so good and helpful she gave her one of the lovely, sugary, candied peel middles to suck.

While Grannie crumbled bread and chopped apples and carrots, she let my sister press the oranges and lemons in the squeezer.

All the time they chattered and laughed and never thought about Bonfire Night. They never noticed the bangs.

Once the black pussy jumped out of the chair and ran and hid himself under the dresser, but they were laughing so much they didn't even notice.

At the very end, Grannie broke a lot of eggs into a basin; then she held the mixer while my sister turned the handle to beat them up.

And sometimes, while they were working, Grannie would make a funny face at my sister, and eat a sultana, and sometimes my sister would make a funny face at Grannie and eat a raisin!

When all the things had been put into the brown bowl, Grannie began to mix and mix with the big spoon. She gave my sister a little wooden spoon so that she could mix too.

Then, Grannie said, 'Now you must
shut your eyes and stir, and make a

wish. You always wish on a Christmas pudding mixture.'

And my sister did. She shut her eyes and turned her spoon round and round. Then Grannie shut her eyes and wished.

My sister said, 'I wished I could come and help you next Bonfire Night, Grannie.'

And Grannie said, 'Well, Missy, that was just what I wished too!'

Then my sister sat quietly by the fire while our grandmother put the pudding mixture into all the basins, and covered them with paper and tied them with cloth.

My sister was very tired now, but she sat smiling and watching until Father came to fetch her.

Our Father said, 'Goodness, Mother, do you still make the Christmas puddings on Bonfire Night? Why, you used to when I was a boy.'

Grannie said, 'This little girl and I think Bonfire Night is the best time of all for making Christmas puddings.'

She said, 'You may as well take your pudding now. It must be boiled all day tomorrow and again on Christmas Day. It should be extra good this year, as I had such a fine helper!'

So Father brought it home that

night and on Christmas Day we had it for dinner.

My sister was so proud when she saw it going into the water on Christmas morning she almost forgot her new toys.

And when we were sitting round the table, and Father poured brandy on it, and lit it, so that the pudding was covered with little blue flames, my sister said, 'Now it's a real bonfire pudding.'

6. Harry's shouting coat

Long ago, when my sister was a funny little girl with a friend called Harry, Harry had an auntie who lived over the sea in Canada, and this auntie used to send Harry presents.

Sometimes she sent him toys, sometimes she sent him sweeties. But once she sent him a very bright coat.

It was the loveliest coat Harry had ever seen. It was the loveliest coat my little sister had ever seen.

It was bright, bright red, and it had a bright, bright yellow collar and bright, bright yellow pockets and shiny goldy buttons and there was white twisty cord round the buttons.

My sister was playing at Harry's house when the coat-parcel came, and they were both very excited.

Harry tried the coat on at once, and walked up and down to show my sister, and then my sister tried it on and walked up and down to show Harry.

But do you know, Harry's mother didn't like that coat at all! She said, 'I really don't think you can wear it to go out in. It's far too loud.'

When she showed the coat to Harry's father, he said, 'Yes, it's loud all right. It shouts.'

Harry's father and mother laughed then. But Harry didn't laugh and my sister didn't laugh. Harry was thoroughly cross. He said, 'It's a very nice coat. Auntie sent it for me. I want to wear it.'

His father said, 'Well, you can wear it in the garden and frighten the birds with it. Then they won't eat all the seeds.'

But Harry didn't want to wear that beautiful coat in the garden. He wanted to wear it where all the other children could see it. My sister wanted him to wear it where all the other children could see it too. She wanted to be with him when everyone was looking at his smart red coat.

She said, 'I think it's a beautiful coat, Harry.'

Harry said, 'I want to wear it outside.' Harry was very cross when he said, 'I want to wear it,' but he didn't shout. He had a little, little cross voice.

Harry had a shouting voice too. He used to shout

at my naughty little sister sometimes, but he had a little, cross voice too.

Harry's mother didn't like to be unkind about the red coat because after all it was Harry's present, so she had a good idea. She said, 'All right, you can wear it out one day if you are a *very good boy*.'

She said this because she thought Harry wouldn't be good.

But he was.

Those two naughty children went out into the garden, and whispered and whispered and they made up their minds that Harry would be good, and he was!

My sister helped him to be good. She didn't quarrel with him or grumble at him. She was good and polite to him, and Harry was good and polite to her. Do you know how they managed it? They played a game of being good and polite people. It was fun!

When Harry was at home he was still good. He helped his father and tidied up his toys, and he kept saying to his mother, 'Haven't I been good enough yet?' Until at last she said Harry could wear his coat tomorrow.

She said she would take Harry and my sister for a picnic on the Island and

Harry could wear his red coat.

Harry and my sister were very pleased about this, because they liked going to the Island very much.

The Island was in the middle of the river. There was an old man in a sailor hat and a blue coat to row you in a boat to the Island, and to come and fetch you later on. He was the ferryman.

It was lovely to sit in the boat with the water all around you. You had to sit very still on the seats or the old man shouted at you. So you couldn't play anything, but it was still very nice.

Sometimes there were lots of people going to the Island, but on this picnic day when Harry wore his loud red coat, there was only Harry's mother, and Harry and my little sister.

The old ferryman wasn't there either. There was just a boy to row the boat. The boy said the old man was his grandad. He said his grandad had gone to get some new teeth, but he would be back later on.

Harry and my sister were disappointed there were no other people going to the Island; they wanted to show off the coat. Lots of people had stared when they went through the town, and they had been very proud. A postman had said, 'My, my!' and a boy had whistled, and some people had come out of a shop to look. It had been exciting.

Harry's mother said she wasn't sorry no one else was going to the Island.

Although there were no other people, Harry and my sister had a lovely time. They ran all round the Island first. Then they played house-on-fire. My sister sat under a bush that was the house, and Harry was the fire-engine and the fireman too in his red coat and shiny buttons.

Then they ate their picnic, and Harry's mother said she would have a little nap before the ferryman came to fetch them. Harry said he would have a nap too, because he had got hot and tired running about in his coat all the time, and my sister said she would have a nap as well as there wouldn't be anyone to play with, so she lay down too, and soon everyone was fast asleep.

Harry's mother woke up first of all, and when she woke up she was very worried. She woke Harry and my sister up, and they were very cross and sleepy at first.

She said, 'Oh, do wake up properly, children. It's late and the boat hasn't come.'

They all ran to look across the river

then, and Harry and my sister forgot to be sleepy because Harry's mother was so worried.

They saw the boat tied up across the river, but there was no boat boy and no old ferryman.

Harry's mother said, 'Oh dear, they have forgotten us!'

When she said this, my sister started to cry, because it sounded so nasty to be forgotten, and then Harry cried too, and his mother had to make a fuss of them until they stopped.

'Never mind,' she said. 'We will wait, and when we see anyone we will call out, and they will know we are here.'

They waited and waited, and, just as they were beginning to think they might have to sleep on the Island all night, they saw the old man in his sailor hat coming down the path by the boat.

They shouted and shouted. But the old man took no notice. They shouted again, but he didn't hear them.

He looked across. He stood still, then he waved and waved to them. He untied the boat, got in it, and began to row and row, straight to the Island.

They were glad to see him.

When he rowed them back, he told Harry's mother that his grandson

449

had forgotten to tell him about them. He said, 'I was just coming to put the boat away.'

Harry's mother said, 'It's a good thing we shouted, then.'

But the old man said, 'I didn't hear any shouting, Mam. I didn't hear anything.'

He said, 'If I hadn't looked across and seen this young chap's coat, I shouldn't have known anyone was here.'

When the old man said this, Harry looked at my little sister and she looked at him. 'Father said the coat shouted,' Harry said.

'It's a good thing it was *loud*,' said

my sister. 'I don't think I would like to sleep on the Island very much.'

When they got home again, Harry's mother said, 'Well, at least you won't get lost in that coat. It's too conspicuous. I think you had better wear it when we go to the park or one of the other places you sometimes get lost in.'

And that is just what Harry did. Sometimes, when they played in the park, he let my sister borrow it for a treat, so that she could run about in the bracken without getting lost.

7. The baby angel

When I was a little girl, and my sister was a little girl, our dear next-door friend Mrs Cocoa Jones was always washing and dusting and polishing her clean, tidy house.

My little sister often went to visit Mrs Jones when she was doing her work. Sometimes she helped her, and sometimes she just sat and watched.

Mr Cocoa Jones was always busy too. He painted and sawed and nailed and glued things. He stuck up wallpaper and mended pipes. When he wasn't doing these things he would go outside and do something new to his garden.

He didn't just plant flowers and vegetables like our father. Oh no! He made pretty paths with big stones, and stuck sea-shells like fans all along the edges. He put a big stone basin on top of a pipe for the birds to bath in, and he made a garden seat for Mrs Cocoa out of twisty branches. My sister used to love watching clever Mr Jones at work.

One day Mr Jones brought home a big barrowful of rocks and stones. He put all these stones in a heap by his back door. Then he put lots of earth on the heap, and planted flowers in the earth.

My sister said, 'What are you doing that for, Mr Cocoa?' and Mr Cocoa said he was making a rockery. He said in the summer, when the flowers were out, it would make a nice bit of colour.

And when the summer came Mr Cocoa's rockery was very beautiful. It was so beautiful that Mother said she would like a rockery too, and Father said he would make one for her next spring.

My sister said she would like a rockery as well, but she didn't wait at all. She went down to the rubbishy end of our garden, and collected lots of bricks and stones and earth and made herself a little rockery right away.

My funny sister made her rockery, but she didn't put flowers on it like Mr Cocoa did. She looked all over our rubbish heap and found pieces of blue glass and red glass and broken china with pretty patterns on it, and she stuck them on her rockery instead.

Mr Cocoa said my sister's rockery was a good idea, because it would be pretty all year round. He said his rockery was only pretty when the flowers were out.

My little sister smiled a lot then, and kind Mr Cocoa said if she wanted any more things for her rockery she could come and look at his rubbish heap, and see if she could find anything. 'Only mind you don't cut yourself on something sharp,' Mr Cocoa said, 'or I'll have Mrs Jones after me!'

My sister found a lot of interesting things for her rockery on the Cocoa Jones's rubbish heap. She found pieces of china and glass, and a piece of an old bubble-pipe. She found one of those diamond-looking, sparkly bottle stoppers, and one of Mr Cocoa's path shells that he had thrown away because he didn't need it. She found half a little crockery dog, and a *round white china thing*, with a pretty little china face on it.

My sister was very pleased with all these things, and she put them on her rockery as well. She put the little half-dog on the top, and the pretty smiling-face thing in front where it smiled and smiled. Everybody said her rockery looked very pretty. Even Father, and he didn't often say things like that.

Well now, one day when my sister went to visit Mrs Cocoa, she found that dear lady very busy. Mrs Cocoa had a very beautiful best front-room, and in this room was a big glass cupboard with all Mrs Cocoa's very best china in it.

When my sister came in, Mrs Cocoa was washing all her lovely china from the glass cupboard, and she said, if my sister would promise not to touch anything, she could come and stand on the stool by the table and watch her.

Mrs Jones had lots of lovely china, and she washed it all very carefully in soapy water, and dried it very, very carefully on an old soft towel. She had plates with roses on, and teapots and vases and little Chinamen, and ladies with fans, and dishes, and tiny red drinking glasses. My sister hadn't seen all these things close to before, but she only looked; she didn't touch a thing!

When Mrs Cocoa was washing a black teapot with yellow daises on it, she said, 'Oh dear! There's something in here!'

My sister looked to see what was in
the teapot, and Mrs Jones showed her

a wet, soapy paper bundle.

'Oh dear,' said Mrs Cocoa. 'I'd forgotten about the baby angel.'

And she carefully opened the wet soapy paper, and inside was a white china baby angel with tiny wings and no clothes on. It was holding a white china basket with white flowers in it.

My sister looked hard at the little angel. She said, 'Oh, poor, poor angel. It hasn't got a head!' And it hadn't.

Mrs Cocoa said, 'All this china came from my old auntie's. The little angel was broken when we unpacked it, but Mr Jones said he would mend it for me.'

Then she told my sister that Mr Cocoa hadn't been able to mend it because the head had disappeared.

Mrs Cocoa said, 'I suppose it must have got burned up when Mr Jones got rid of all the paper the china was wrapped in. It's such a shame. I always loved that little angel when I was a girl!'

My sister looked hard at that baby angel, and then she remembered something. She remembered the round china white thing with the pretty smiling face that she had put on her rockery.

She didn't say a word to Mrs

Cocoa. She slipped off the stool, and ran out of the house, through her own little gate, up our garden, straight to her rockery and back again.

'Here it is, Mrs Cocoa. Here it is,' my sister said. 'Here's the baby angel's head. It was on my rockery.'

Mrs Cocoa Jones was delighted. She ran in to tell Mother about my sister's cleverness in finding the baby angel's little head. She told Mr Jones when he came home, and he got out his sticky glue and stuck it on at once. It looked very pretty when it was mended.

Mrs Cocoa took the baby angel in to show my sister, and my sister saw that it was smiling at the basket of white flowers.

'You are a good, clever child!' Mrs Cocoa said. She said that if my sister hadn't been so clever and made such a lovely rockery she would never have found the angel's head. She said it must have fallen out of the paper when Mr Cocoa burned the rubbish many years ago.

Mrs Cocoa said, 'I prize that little angel very much.' But she said that when my sister was a lady of twenty-one she would give her the baby angel for her very own! Wasn't that kind of her?

She did too, and if you go to my good, grown-up sister's house you will see the baby angel smiling at his flowers on my sister's mantelpiece.

More Naughty Little Sister Stories

Contents

1. The very first story

A very long time ago, when I was a little girl, I didn't have a naughty little sister at all. I was a child all on my own. I had a father and a mother of course, but I hadn't any other little brothers or sisters – I was quite alone.

I was a very lucky little girl because I had a dear grannie and a dear grandad and lots of kind aunts and uncles to make a fuss of me. They played games with me, and gave me toys and took me for walks, and bought me ice-creams and told me stories, but I hadn't got a little sister.

Well now, one day, when I was a child on my own, I went to stay with my kind godmother-aunt in the country. My kind godmother-aunt was very good to me. She took me out every day to see the farm animals and to pick flowers, and she read stories to me, and let me cook little cakes and jam tarts in her oven, and I was very, very happy. I didn't want to go home one bit.

Then, one day, my godmother-aunt said, 'Here is a letter from your father, and what do you think he says?'

My aunt was smiling and smiling.

'What do you think he says?' she asked. 'He says that you have a little baby sister waiting for you at home!'

I *was* excited! I said, 'I think I had better go home at once, don't you?' and my kind godmother-aunt said, 'I think you had indeed.' And she took me home that very day!

My aunt took me on a train and a bus and another bus, and then I was home!

And, do you know, before I'd even got indoors, I heard a waily-waily noise coming from the house, and my godmother-aunt said, 'That is your new sister.'

'Waah-waah,' my little sister was saying, 'waah-waah.'

I was surprised to think that such a very new child could make so much noise, and I ran straight indoors and straight upstairs and straight into my mother's bedroom. And there was my good kind mother sitting up in bed smiling and smiling, and there, in a

cot that used to be my old cot, was my new cross little sister crying and crying!

My mother said, 'Sh-sh, baby, here is your big sister come to see you.' My mother lifted my naughty little baby sister out of the cot, and my little sister stopped crying at once.

My mother said, 'Come and look.'

My little sister was wrapped up in a big woolly white shawl, and my mother undid the shawl and there was my little sister! When my mother put her down on the bed, my little sister began to cry again.

She was a little, little red baby,

crying and crying.

'Waah-waah, waah-waah,' – like that.
Isn't it a nasty noise?

My little sister had tiny hands and
tiny little feet. She went on crying
and crying, and curling up her toes,
and beating with her arms in a very
cross way.

My mother said, 'She likes being
lifted up and cuddled. She is a very
good baby when she is being cuddled
and fussed, but when I put her down
she cries and cries. She is an artful
pussy,' my mother said.

I was very sorry to see my little
sister crying, and I was disappointed

because I didn't want a crying little sister very much, but I went and looked at her. I looked at her little red face and her little screwed up eyes and her little crying mouth and then I said, 'Don't cry, baby, don't cry, baby.'

And, do you know, when I said, 'Don't cry, baby,' my little sister *stopped crying*, really stopped crying at once. For me! Because *I* told her to. She opened her eyes and she looked and looked and she didn't cry any more.

My mother said, 'Just fancy! She must know you are her own big sister! She has stopped crying.'

I was pleased to think that my little sister had stopped crying because she knew I was her big sister, and I put my finger on my sister's tiny, tiny hand and my little sister caught hold of my finger tight with her little curly fingers.

My mother said I could hold my little sister on my lap if I was careful. So I sat down on a chair and my godmother-aunt put my little sister on to my lap, and I held her very carefully; and my little sister didn't cry at all. She went to sleep like a good baby.

And do you know, she was so small and so sweet and she held my finger so tightly with her curly little fingers that I loved her and loved her and although she often cried after that I never minded it a bit, because I knew how nice and cuddly she could be when she was good!

2. My Naughty Little Sister and the book-little-boy

Do you like having stories read to you? When I was a little girl I used to like it very much. My little sister liked it too, but she pretended that she didn't.

When my sister and I were very little children we had a kind aunt who used to come and read stories to us. She used to read all the stories that she'd had read to her when *she* was a little girl.

I used to listen and listen and say, 'Go on! Go on!' whenever my auntie stopped for a minute, but my little sister used to pretend that she wasn't listening. Wasn't she silly? She used to fidget with her old doll, Rosy-Primrose, and pretend that she was playing babies with her, but really she listened and listened too, and heard every word.

Do you know how I knew that she listened and listened? I'll tell you. When my little sister was in bed at night she used to tell the stories all over again to Rosy-Primrose.

One day when my aunt came to read to us, she said, 'I've got a book here that I won as a Sunday School prize. I used to like these stories when I was a child, I hope you will like them too.'

So our aunt read us a story about a poor little boy. It was a very sad story in the beginning because this poor little boy was very ragged and hungry. It said that he had no breakfast and no dinner and no supper, but it was lovely at the end because a nice kind lady took him home with her and said she was his real mother and gave him lots of nice things to eat and lots of nice clothes to wear, and a white pony. But the 'nothing to eat' part was very sad.

Now, you know, my little sister liked eating, and she was so surprised to hear about the book-little-boy with nothing to eat that she forgot to pretend that she wasn't listening and she said, 'No breakfast?' She said 'no breakfast' in a very little voice.

Our auntie said, 'No, no breakfast.'

My little sister said, 'No dinner?' She said that in a little voice too, because she thought no dinner and no breakfast was terrible.

My aunt said, 'No dinner, *and* no supper,' and she was so pleased to think that my funny little sister *had* been listening that she said, 'Would you like to see the picture?' And my little sister said 'please' and I said 'please' too.

So our kind aunt showed us the

picture in the book that went with the poor little boy story. It was a very miserable picture because the little boy was sitting all alone in the corner of a room, looking very sad. There was an empty plate on the floor beside this poor little boy, and under the picture it said, '*Nothing to eat.*'

Wasn't that sad?

My little sister thought it was very sad. She looked and looked at the picture and she said, '*No* breakfast, *no* dinner, and *no* supper.' Like that, over and over again.

My aunt said, 'Cheer up. He had lots to eat when his kind rich mother

took him home in the end; he had a
pony too, remember,' my aunt said.

But my sister said, 'No *picture*
dinner. Poor, poor boy,' she said.

Well now, when the reading time

was over my little sister was a very quiet child. She was very quiet when she had her supper. She sat by the fire and my mother gave her a big piece of buttery bread and a big mug of warm sweet milk, but she was very quiet, she said, 'thank you' in a tiny quiet voice, and she drank up her milk like a good child. When my mother came to say that the hot-water bottle was in her bed, she said her prayers at once and went straight upstairs.

My mother kissed my warm little sister and said 'good night' to her, and my little sister said 'good night'. But when my kind aunt kissed her and said, 'good night' to her, my little sister said, '*No* breakfast, *no* dinner,' and my auntie said, 'No supper,' but my little sister smiled and said, '*yes, supper.*' My little sister looked very smiley and pleased with herself.

When our aunt went to go home, and looked for the Sunday School prize-book, she knew why my little sister had said such a funny thing.

Do you know what that silly child had done? She had put her piece of buttery bread inside the Sunday School prize-book, on top of the little book boy's picture.
She had given her

supper to the book-little-boy!

Of course the book was very greasy and crumby after that, which was a pity because our aunt had kept it very tidy indeed as it had been a prize. I suppose it was a very naughty thing to have done.

But my little sister hadn't *meant* to be naughty. She thought that she had given the book-little-boy her own supper, and you know she was quite a greedy child, so it was a kind thing to do really.

Now you know why she said, '*No* breakfast, *no* dinner, and *yes, supper,*' don't you?

3. My Naughty Little Sister and poor Charlie Cocoa

In the days when I was a little girl, and my naughty little sister was a very small child, my little sister often helped Mrs Cocoa Jones to do her housework. Mrs Cocoa worked *so* hard, and had *such* a clean and tidy house, that she was glad when my little sister came to help her.

Mrs Cocoa Jones had a shiny red dustpan and a brush with a red handle, and because my little sister was such a helpful child, Mrs Cocoa bought her a nice little shiny red dustpan and a little brush with a red handle for herself. Wasn't that very kind of her?

Mrs Cocoa hung her dustpan and brush on a hook behind her broom-cupboard door when she wasn't using them, and dear Mr Cocoa put another hook behind the broom-cupboard door so that my little sister could hang her dustpan and brush there too. It was a nice low hook so that my little sister could reach it all by herself. What a smiley pleased girl she was when she saw her own little dustpan and brush hanging underneath Mrs Cocoa's big dustpan and brush!

'Now we shall *work* and *work*, Mrs Cocoa,' my little sister said.

When Mrs Cocoa swept her carpets, she knelt on the floor and brushed the dust into her dustpan, and my little sister knelt on the floor too, and brushed the dust into *her* dustpan. *Sweep sweep* went Mrs Cocoa's big brush and *sweep sweep* went my little sister's small brush. 'Aren't we busy, Mrs Cocoa?' said my little sister as she brushed and brushed.

Mrs Cocoa would sit up and say, 'Oh! My *poor* back!' and my naughty little sister would sit up and say, 'Oh, *my* poor back!' and then they would

carry their pans of dust out to the dustbin and grumble and grumble about hard work.

My little sister was only pretending to grumble, because she liked helping Mrs Cocoa and her back wasn't really bad at all, but poor Mrs Cocoa really was grumbling when she said, 'Oh my *poor* back!'

Now, kind Mr Cocoa was very worried about Mrs Cocoa's poor back, so one day he took some money out of his savings and bought Mrs Cocoa a fine vacuum cleaner.

Mrs Cocoa was pleased! She had never had a vacuum cleaner before, and when Mr Cocoa fixed it up for her, and showed her how quickly it worked, she was very excited.

Mrs Cocoa was so excited that she hurried out into her back-garden, and called to my little sister who was playing in our garden. 'Come and see what Mr Jones has bought for me!' she called and my little sister ran and fetched her dolly, Rosy-Primrose, to see too.

Then my little sister hurried through her very own little gate into Mr Cocoa's garden, then through the back door into Mrs Cocoa's shiny-clean kitchen. *Then my little sister stopped.* She stood still and *listened.*

There was a funny, humming noise coming from Mrs Cocoa's sitting-room, and my little sister didn't like it.

'Come in,' said Mrs Cocoa, 'come and see my new cleaner.'

Then my little sister walked

forward and looked in at the sitting-room door. She had never seen a vacuum cleaner before, so she stared and stared and listened and listened. And she didn't like it one bit!

'I don't like it!' said my naughty little sister. 'I want to go home!'

Then Mr Cocoa switched off the cleaner and the noise stopped, but my little sister still didn't like it. 'I want to go home,' she said.

'But it's to help poor Mrs Cocoa do her work,' said Mr Cocoa in his nice kind voice. 'It will eat all the nasty dust for her.'

'I help Mrs Cocoa do the work!'

said my sister. '*I* help Mrs Cocoa do the work!' and she began to cry, and cry, and she ran right out of Mrs Cocoa's tidy clean house and back to our house, crying and crying. *And she wouldn't go to see Mrs Cocoa at all.*

My little sister would not go into Mrs Cocoa's house for a long while, and, if she heard the cleaner working when she was playing in our garden she ran straight in to our mother and hid her face in our mother's apron, because she didn't like the noise the cleaner made.

Now Mrs Cocoa Jones was very very sad when my little sister wouldn't come to see her, because she loved my bad little sister very much. The vacuum cleaner did a lot of work for Mrs Cocoa, and her bad back was a good deal better, but Mrs Cocoa was still sad. So she spoke to Mr Cocoa, and he said he would have a word with my little sister and see if he could make her like the vacuum after all.

One morning when Mr Cocoa was digging his garden, and my little sister was blowing some of the lovely white fluffy seeds from a dandelion flower, Mr Cocoa said, 'I should think our Charlie would like some of that fluff.'

My little sister was surprised to

hear Mr Cocoa say this because she didn't know anything about Charlie.

'Poor Charlie gets so hungry,' said Mr Cocoa Jones, 'and all we can give him to eat is dust and dirt – and he does love some nice fluff if he can get it.'

'What Charlie?' said my little sister. 'What Charlie is hungry?'

'Charlie the cleaner,' said clever Mr Cocoa. 'Charlie who eats the dirt for Mrs Cocoa. There's not a lot of dirt in our house you know,' he said, 'poor old Charlie.'

Mr Cocoa spoke so nicely that Charlie sounded just like a poor hungry boy and my little sister felt quite sorry about him. So she gave Mr Cocoa the dandelion flower seeds and said, 'For Charlie,' and Mr Cocoa took them indoors.

Then my little sister heard the sound of Mrs Cocoa's cleaner, but this time she didn't run indoors, she stood and listened to the sound poor Charlie made when he ate the dandelion fluff and she was quite glad to think that she had given it to him.

When Mr Cocoa came out again, my little sister said, 'Did Charlie like it?' and Mr Cocoa said, 'Yes, it was a treat for him.' So then my little sister went up and down the garden and picked a lot of dandelion clocks for Charlie.

'Why don't you come and give them to him?' said Mr Cocoa. 'Come and see him eat them all up. Poor old Charlie,' Mr Cocoa said.

'Poor old Charlie,' said my little sister, and because she was quite sorry for poor Charlie, she went into Mrs Cocoa's house to see him.

When my little sister really looked at poor Charlie she wasn't a bit frightened. She saw that he had a round shiny body and a long trunk-thing. There was a shiny handle fixed to Charlie's trunk that had a black mouth-looking thing at the end of it.

'Hello, Charlie Cocoa,' said my little sister, 'you are a funny-looking boy.'

When Mr Cocoa switched on Charlie's noise, my little sister didn't like it at all, but she wasn't frightened any more. She laughed and put her hands over her ears, and watched as Charlie ate up all the dandelion seeds. He was hungry! My little sister knew that there *wouldn't* be very much for him on Mrs Cocoa's clean floors. She knew that you had to do a great deal of brushing to get even a little dust from those carpets.

My little sister was so sorry for

Charlie, that, can you ever guess what she did? She went to Mr Cocoa's broom cupboard, and got out her own little dustpan and brush, and then she went out into Mrs Cocoa's garden, and swept up a nice pan of dust from the path, and brought it in and gave it to him.

'There, Charlie, eat it up do,' my little sister said. 'Poor Charlie! Poor Charlie Cocoa!'

4. My Naughty Little Sister and the big girl's bed

A long time ago, when my naughty little sister was a very small girl, she had a nice cot with pull-up sides so that she couldn't fall out and bump herself.

My little sister's cot was a very pretty one. It was pink, and had pictures of fairies and bunny-rabbits painted on it.

It had been my old cot when I was a very small child and I had taken care of the pretty pictures. I used to kiss the fairies 'good night' when I went to bed, but my bad little sister did not kiss them and take care of their pictures. Oh no!

My naughty little sister did dreadful things to those poor fairies. She scribbled on them with pencils and scratched them with tin-lids, and knocked them with poor old Rosy-Primrose her doll, until there were hardly any pictures left at all. She said, 'Nasty fairies. Silly old rabbits.'

There! Wasn't she a bad child? You wouldn't do things like that, would you?

And my little sister jumped and jumped on her cot. After she had been tucked up at night-time she would get out from under the covers, and jump and jump. And when she woke up in the morning she jumped and jumped again, until one day, when she was jumping, the bottom fell right out of the cot, and my naughty little sister, and the mattress, and the covers, and poor Rosy-Primrose all fell out on to the floor!

Then our mother said, 'That child must have a bed!' Even though our father managed to mend the cot, our mother said, 'She must have a bed!'

My naughty little sister said, 'A big bed for me?'

And our mother said, 'I am afraid so, you bad child. You are too rough now for your poor old cot.'

My little sister wasn't ashamed of being too rough for her cot. She was pleased because she was going to have a new bed, and she said, 'A big girl's bed for me!'

My little sister told everybody that she was going to have a big girl's bed.

She told her kind friend the window-cleaner man, and the coalman, and the milkman. She told the dustman too. She said, 'You can have my old cot soon, dustman, because I am going to have a big girl's bed.' And she was as pleased as pleased.

But our mother wasn't pleased at all. She was rather worried. You see, our mother was afraid that my naughty little sister would jump and jump on her new bed, and scratch it, and treat it badly. My naughty little sister had done such dreadful things to her old cot, that my mother was afraid she would spoil the new bed too.

Well now, my little sister told the lady who lived next door all about her new bed. The lady who lived next door to us was called Mrs Jones, but my little sister used to call her Mrs Cocoa Jones because she used to go in and have a cup of cocoa with her every morning.

Mrs Cocoa Jones was a very kind lady, and when she heard about the new bed she said, 'I have a little yellow eiderdown and a yellow counterpane upstairs, and they are too small for any of my beds, so when your new bed comes, I will give them to you.'

My little sister was excited, but when

she told our mother what Mrs Cocoa had said, our mother shook her head.

'Oh, dear,' she said, 'what will happen to the lovely eiderdown and counterpane when our bad little girl has them?'

Then, a kind aunt who lived near us said, 'I have a dear little green nightie-case put away in a drawer. It belonged to me when I was a little girl. When your new bed comes you can have it to put your nighties in like a big girl.'

My little sister said, 'Good. Good,' because of all the nice things she was going to have for her bed. But our mother was more worried than ever.

She said, 'Oh dear! That pretty nightie-case. You'll spoil it, I know you will!'

But my little sister went on being pleased as pleased about it.

Then one day the new bed arrived. It was a lovely shiny brown bed, new as new, with a lovely blue stripy mattress to go on it: new as new. And there was a new stripy pillow too. Just like a real big girl would have.

My little sister watched while my mother took the poor old cot to pieces, and stood it up against the wall. She watched when the new bed was put up, and the new mattress was laid on top of it. She watched the new pillow being put into a clean white case, and when our mother made the bed with clean new sheets and clean new blankets, she said, 'Really big-girl! A big girl's bed – all for me.'

Then Mrs Cocoa Jones came in, and she was carrying the pretty yellow eiderdown and the yellow counterpane. They were very shiny and satiny like buttercup flowers, and when our mother put them on top of the new bed, they looked beautiful.

Then our kind aunt came down the road, and *she* was carrying a little parcel, and in the little parcel was the pretty green nightie-case. My little sister ran down the road to meet her because she was so excited. She was more excited still when our aunt picked up her little nightdress and put it into the pretty green case and laid the green case on the yellow shiny eiderdown.

My little sister was so pleased that

she was glad when bedtime came.

And, what do you think? She got carefully, carefully into bed with Rosy-Primrose, and she laid herself down and stretched herself out – carefully, carefully like a good, nice girl.

And she didn't jump and jump, and she didn't scratch the shiny brown wood, or scribble with pencils or scrape with tin-lids. Not ever! Not even when she had had the new bed a long, long time.

My little sister took great care of her big girl's bed. She took great care of her shiny yellow eiderdown and counterpane and her pretty green nightie-case.

And whatever do you think she said to me?

She said, 'You had the fairy pink cot before I did. But this is my very own big girl's bed, and I am going to take great care of my very own bed, like a big girl!'

5. The cross photograph

A long time ago, when I was a little girl with a naughty little sister who was younger than myself, our mother made us a beautiful coat each.

They were lovely red coats with black buttons to do them up with and curly-curly black fur on them to keep us warm. We were very proud children when we put our new red coats on.

Our mother was proud too, because she had never made any coats before, and she said, 'I know! You shall have your photographs taken. Then we can always remember how smart they look.'

So our proud mother took my naughty little sister and me to have our photographs taken in our smart red coats.

The man in the photographer's shop was very smart too. He had curly-curly black hair *just* like the fur on our new coats, and he had a pink flower in his buttonhole and a yellow handkerchief that he waved and waved when he took our photographs.

There were lots of pictures in the shop. There were pictures of children, and ladies being married, and ladies smiling, and gentlemen smiling, and pussy-cats with long fur, and black-and-white rabbits. All those pictures! And the smart curly-curly man had taken every one himself!

He said we could go and look at his pictures while he talked to our mother, so I went round and looked at them. But do you know, my naughty little sister wouldn't look. She stood still as still and quiet as quiet, and she shut her eyes.

Yes, she did. She shut her eyes and wouldn't look at anything. She was being a stubborn girl, and when the photographer-man said, 'Are you both ready?' my bad little sister kept her eyes shut and said, '*No.*'

Our mother said, 'But surely you want your photograph taken?'

But my naughty little sister kept her eyes shut tight as tight, and said, 'No taken! No taken!' And she got so cross, and shouted so much, that the curly man said, 'All right then. I will just take your big sister by herself.'

'I will take a nice photograph of your big sister,' said the photographer-man, 'and she will be able to show it to all her friends. Wouldn't you like a photograph of yourself to show to your friends?'

My naughty little sister did want a

photograph of herself to show to her friends, but she would not say so. She just said, 'No photograph!'

So our mother said, 'Oh well, it looks as if it will be only one picture then, for we can't keep this gentleman waiting all day.'

So the photographer-man made me stand on a box-thing. There was a little table on the box-thing, and I had to put my hand on the little table and stand up straight and smile.

There was a beautiful picture of a garden on the wall behind me. It was such a big picture that when the photograph was taken it looked just as if I was standing in a real garden. Wasn't that a clever idea?

When I was standing quite straight and quite smiley, the curly photographer-man shone a lot of bright lights, and then he got his big black camera-on-legs and said, 'Watch for the dickey-bird!' And he waved and waved his yellow handkerchief. And then 'click!' said the camera, and my picture was safe inside it.

'That's all,' said the man, and he helped me to get down.

Now, what do you think? While the man was taking my picture, my little sister had opened her eyes to peep, and when she saw me standing all straight and smiley in my beautiful new coat, and heard the man say, 'Watch for the dickey-bird,' and saw him wave his yellow handkerchief, she stared and stared.

The man said, 'That was all right, wasn't it?' and I said, 'Yes, thank you.'

Then the curly man looked at my little sister and he saw that her eyes weren't shut any more so he said, 'Are you going to change your mind now?'

And what do you think? My little sister changed her mind. She stopped being stubborn. She changed her mind and said, 'Yes, please,' like a good polite child. You see, she hadn't known anything about photographs before, and she had been frightened, but when she saw me having my picture taken, and had seen how easy it was, she hadn't been frightened any more.

She let the man lift her on to the box-thing. She was so small though, that he took the table away and found a little chair for her to sit on, and gave her a teddy-bear to hold.

Then he said, 'Smile nicely now,' and my naughty little sister smiled very beautifully indeed.

The man said, 'Watch for the dickey-bird,' and he waved his yellow handkerchief to her, and 'click', my naughty little sister's photograph had been taken too!

But what do you think? *She hadn't kept smiling*. When the photographs came home for us to look at, there was my little sister holding the teddy-bear and looking as cross as cross.

Our mother *was* surprised, she said, 'I thought the man told you to *smile*!'

And what do think that funny girl said? She said, 'I did smile, but there wasn't any dickey-bird, so I stopped.'

My mother said, 'Oh dear! We shall have to have it taken all over again!'

But our father said, 'No, I like this one. It is such a natural picture. I like it as it is.' And he laughed and laughed and laughed and laughed.

My little sister liked the cross picture very much too, and sometimes, when she hadn't anything else to do, she climbed up to the looking-glass and made cross faces at herself. *Just* like the cross face in the photograph!

6. My Naughty Little Sister
wins a prize

A long time ago, when I was a little girl, my naughty little sister, who was smaller than me, had a lot of friends, but her favourite friends were the nice coalman, and the nice milkman, and the baker with a poor bad leg, and the window-cleaner man, and her very, very favourite friend was called Mr Blakey and he had a shoe-mending shop, and had rather a cross and roary voice.

Now one day everyone where we lived became very excited, because they heard that the town was going to have a Grand Carnival.

Everyone talked and talked about the Carnival because the town had never had a Carnival before, and there were pictures of funny clowns with writing underneath in all the shop windows and stuck up on all the fences. The clown was to show how jolly and funny the Grand Carnival was going to be, and the writing was to tell about all the nice things that would be happening when Carnival Day came.

My little sister liked the clown-picture very much, and because she

wasn't old enough to read, she asked
our mother to tell her what the writing
was about, and she asked questions
and questions.

My mother told her that all the
shops would be shut and there would
be swings and roundabouts in the
park, and a band.

My little sister asked more
questions and questions, and my
father told her that there would be pony-
rides and toe-dancing and fireworks
and a flower-show.

But my little sister still asked
questions and questions until at last
our father and mother said, 'You must

wait and see for yourself when Carnival Day comes.'

Well now, there was one thing about the Grand Carnival that my little sister liked to hear best of all, and that was the Grand Procession and Fancy Dress Parade.

Do you know what that means? It means that lots of people dress up in beautiful clothes or funny clothes and they go through all the streets of the town so that everyone can see them. Some of the people walk, and some ride in cars or on lorries or bicycles, and the people who look the most beautiful or the funniest, win prizes.

Do you know why my little sister was so interested in the Grand Procession and Fancy Dress Parade? It was because all her special friends were going to be in it.

When the nice coalman came, he told my naughty little sister that he was going to wash down the coal-cart and put lovely red ribbons on his horse, and that all the Infant School children were going to ride with him. He said that the Infant School children were going to be dressed up as fairies and pixies. The nice coalman said that *he* wasn't going to be a fairy or a pixie, but that he was going to wear his Sunday-best hat, so, of course, my little sister wanted to see him very much.

The nice milkman said he was going to have lots of flags on his cart, and that all the pretty ladies from the dairy shop were going to be dressed up to look like milkmaids, and walk beside it with milking pails. The milkman said that he was going to be dressed up, too.

When my little sister asked the milkman what he was going to be dressed up *as*, the milkman said, 'Ah! Just you wait and see! I'll be very fancy, I promise you!'

That sounded so exciting that my little sister wanted to see *him* very much indeed.

The nice baker said that he was going to leave his cart at home because he was going to march *with his medals up* with the other old soldiers. That did sound grand – 'march with his medals up'.

My little sister could hardly wait to see the nice baker marching with his poor bad leg along with all the other old soldiers, and she told the nice baker that she would keep a very special look-out for *him*.

When the window-cleaner man

came, he said that he was going to dress his barrow up with roses and roses, and that his little niece was going to be a rose-fairy on the top. Didn't that sound pretty? My little sister thought it did, and she said, 'I wish the Grand Carnival Day would hurry up!'

My little sister was so pleased and so excited about the Carnival that she went in to see her dear friend Mr Blakey at the shoe-mending shop to see what *he* was going to dress up as.

But Mr Blakey said he was too old for dressing up and being a poppy-show. He said that if everyone dressed

up and walked in the Grand
Procession there wouldn't be anyone
to watch it, and then there would
be no reason for dressing up at all.
Mr Blakey said he was going to be
a spectator.

My naughty little sister did not
know what 'spectator' meant so Mr

Blakey said it meant someone who looked on.

So my little sister said, 'I will be a Spectator too, and Mother will be a Spectator, and Father will be a Spectator, and my big sister will be a Spectator.' And she was very pleased indeed.

But my naughty little sister wasn't a spectator. No, she was *something else*.

This is what happened.

The day before the Grand Carnival Day, the window-cleaner man came to our house. He didn't bring his barrow, he came on a bicycle and looked very worried.

The window-cleaner man told my mother that his little niece was not a well girl, and that she had got to stay in bed for a few days. He said she wouldn't be able to be the rose-fairy on his barrow after all, and he asked my mother if she would let my little sister ride on his barrow instead. He said that my little sister was just the same size as his little niece, so that the rose-fairy frock would fit her nicely.

Wasn't that a lovely idea? It was very sad about the poor little not-well niece wasn't it? But it was lovely for my naughty little sister.

My little sister said, 'Please let me,

please. *Please* do.'

My mother said, 'I don't know. You do get into such dreadful mischief.'

But the window-cleaner man said, 'She can't come to any harm on the barrow.'

And my little sister said, 'I will be good – I will be very, very good. I *promise*.'

So at last my mother said, 'Well, if it's a fine day tomorrow, she may go.'

The window-cleaner man and my little sister were both very pleased when our mother said this, and they were more pleased still next morning, when they saw the bright sunshine, and knew that it was going to be a fine day.

So, my little sister was dressed up in the beautiful rose-fairy dress that the poor little ill niece had been going to wear, and it was a perfect fit.

The rose-fairy dress was pink, and sticking out, and it had dear little green wings – just like leaves.

When my little sister was dressed she ran through her own little gate in the back-garden to see Mr and Mrs Cocoa Jones who lived next door, to show them how smart she was, and Mrs Cocoa said that she looked just like a real fairy.

My naughty little sister was so pleased that she danced a special little made-up dance for them. She would have danced for a long time, only my mother called, 'Hurry up, or the Parade will start without you.'

So my little sister went off with my mother through the town to the place that the procession was to start from, and everyone stared as they went by, to see such a very pretty rose-fairy in the street, and my little sister held tight to Mother's hand and looked very pleased and smiley. She was a proud girl!

She was prouder still when she saw the window-cleaning barrow, because it looked so beautiful. It was covered with so many beautiful roses that you couldn't see that it was a barrow at all, and there was a dear little chair made of roses for my little sister to sit on, and a sunshade of rose-petals for her to hold.

(They weren't real roses, of course – they were made of paper, but they looked *very* real. I thought you would be wondering about the prickles if I didn't explain this.)

The window-cleaner man had a smart white coat on, and a new straw hat, with a rose in his button-hole, and he was very glad to see how pretty my sister looked. 'You are a credit to your family,' he said to her, and he lifted her up very carefully into the little chair, and our mother spread out her sticking-out skirt, and tidied her wings and made her look really lovely.

While she was waiting for the parade to start, she looked at all the other fancy-dressed people, and they were all very lovely too. She saw her friend the coalman with his cart. He looked very clean and nice – not a bit coaly today, and his cart had lots of tree-branches tied all over it, and all the Infant School children were in the cart, laughing and shouting, and waving their fairy wands. The coalman didn't see my little sister, because he was walking along beside the horse, but she saw him and his Sunday best hat, too.

My little sister saw her friend the milkman as well, although he looked so funny that she hardly knew him, but she knew his cart, and she knew the young ladies from the shop – even though they were all dressed up as milkmaids! The milkman had a tall black hat like a chimney-pot, and his nose was painted red, and he looked a little bit like the clown on the Grand Carnival pictures. The milkman saw my little sister and he waved to her. But my little sister didn't wave back, she sat still and quiet, because she wanted to be good today.

She didn't see the baker because all the Old Soldiers were walking at the front of the parade, behind the band, but she saw lots of other old soldiers with their medals up, and they all looked so smart and nice, and their medals were so shiny, that she knew the poor bad-leg baker must be looking very grand indeed.

Then the band began to play, and the procession started. The window-cleaner man said, 'Ups-adaisy', and

he took up the handles of his barrow –
that you couldn't see for roses
and roses – and off they went, and
everyone saw my pretty little rose-
fairy sister, with her dress spread
out nicely, and her leafy little wings
sticking up quite straight – looking as
good as gold.

Mr Blakey hadn't known that my
little sister was going to be in the
procession, and he *was* surprised when
he saw her going by. He waved and
waved, and said, 'Bravo-hooray,' until
my little sister saw him. When she did,
she waved to him and blew him a little
kiss, and then she sat good and still

again, while the window-cleaner man
pushed and pushed.

And what do you think? When the
Grand Procession and Fancy Dress
Parade was over, the window-cleaner
man got a first prize for his beautiful
rose barrow. And my little sister was

given a special prize for looking so beautiful and being so good.

The window-cleaner man had a little wooden clock for his prize, and my little sister had a baby doll with shutting eyes and a long white dress.

The window-cleaner man said that my little sister had been a thoroughly good child, and when my little sister thanked him for taking her, he said it was a treat to have her with him.

Then she did a kind and generous thing, she did it all her own self, without anyone telling her to. My little sister remembered that poor ill little niece who couldn't wear the nice dress or go in the parade – so she gave the shutting-eye doll to the window-cleaner man and asked him to give it to his poor ill niece, who couldn't be in the procession. Wasn't that nice of her?

My little sister said she was very, very sorry about the ill little niece, but that she was very glad all the same to have been in the Grand Procession.

The window-cleaner man said that next time there was a Carnival, he would put two little chairs on his barrow, and then my little sister and his little niece could be fairies together.

7. My Naughty Little Sister and the baby

One day, long ago, when I was a little girl and my naughty little sister was a very little girl, a lady called Mrs Rogers asked my mother if she would mind her little boy-baby for the afternoon.

My mother was very pleased to help Mrs Rogers. 'I should be glad to mind the baby,' she said.

I was very pleased to think we were going to have a little boy-baby in our house for a whole afternoon, but my little sister said, 'I don't know babies, do I?'

Our mother said, 'No, but I expect you will know this one quite well by the time Mrs Rogers comes for it. You can't help knowing babies,' our mother said.

And my little sister said, 'Well, I hope I am glad when I know it.'

Well now, when Mrs Rogers came, my silly sister would not go out to look at the baby, she stood at the door and behaved in a very shy and peepy way and waited for our mother to call her.

'Come and look at the boy-baby,' said Mother, and she took my sister by the hand to look at the baby in the pram.

He was a very dear baby. He was kicking and cooing and smiling and looking very happy.

'Isn't he nice?' my mother said.

My little sister didn't say, 'Yes, he is nice,' because she didn't know the baby very well then, she said, 'He's very fat.'

My mother told my little sister, 'All babies are fat. *You* were fat too,' she said.

My little sister was very surprised to hear that she had been fat like the boy-baby. She stuck out her tummy and blew out her cheeks to look fat, and said, 'Fat girl.'

When the baby saw my little sister pretending to be fat, he began to laugh, and when he laughed he showed a little white tooth. 'Look, a toothy,' said my little sister, and when she said, 'Look, a toothy', that little boy-baby laughed very loudly indeed, and he took off his white woolly cap and he threw it right out of the pram!

My little sister picked up the white woolly cap for the baby.

'Put it back on his head,' our mother said, and my little sister did put it back on his head, and do you know, the bad boy-baby pulled his cap straight off again and threw it out of the pram!

So – my little sister picked the cap up *again* – and put it on the boy-baby's head *again*, and that naughty boy pulled it off and threw it away and laughed and laughed, and my little sister laughed as well because the boy-baby was so jolly and so fat.

Then my little sister talked to the baby, 'You must keep your cap *on*,' she said, and she pulled it on very carefully and tightly, and when he tried to pull it off again it only fell over one of his eyes.

Then my little sister put his cap straight, and *then* she did a very clever thing to make him forget all about his cap. She popped her old doll, Rosy-Primrose, round the side of the pram, and said, 'Boh!' And the boy-baby was so pleased he giggled and giggled.

So my little sister popped Rosy-Primrose round the pram again and again, and each time the funny baby giggled and my little sister giggled. Mother laughed and I laughed too to see my funny sister and the funny boy-baby.

Then my little sister said to the boy-baby, 'What is your name?' and the boy-baby laughed again and said, 'Ay-ay.'

'Where do you live?' asked my little sister, and the boy-baby said, 'Ay-ay' again. Then the baby said, 'Oigle, oigle, oigle,' and my sister said, 'That's a funny thing to say.'

My mother said, 'He doesn't talk properly yet. *You* didn't talk when you were a baby.'

What a surprise for my naughty little sister. 'Not talk!'

When tea-time came the baby sat in

the old high-chair next to my naughty little sister, and my mother gave him some crusts with butter on them.

That bad baby dropped some of his crusts on the floor, and sucked some of them, and waved some of them about, and then he tried to push a crust into my little sister's ear. She was cross!

But our mother told her that the

baby was too little to know any better, so my little sister forgave the baby and laughed at him.

When tea was over, the baby lay in his pram and played with his toes, and then he fell asleep. He was fast asleep when Mrs Rogers came to take him home.

When my naughty little sister went to bed that night, do you know what she did? She pretended that she couldn't talk, she said, 'Ay-ay, ay-ay,' and played with her toes just like the boy-baby did.

Then she *did* speak, she said, 'I know lots about babies now, don't I?'

8. Bad Harry's haircut

Quite a long time ago, when I was a little girl, my naughty little sister used to play with a little boy called Harry.

This boy Harry only lived a little way away from us, and as there were no nasty roads to cross between our houses, Harry used to come all on his own to play with my little sister, and she used to go all on her own to play with him. And they were Very Good Friends.

And they were both very naughty children. Oh dear!

But, if you could have seen this Bad Harry you wouldn't have said that he was a naughty child. He looked so very good. Yes, he looked very good indeed.

My little sister never looked very good, even when she was behaving herself, but Bad Harry looked good all the time.

My naughty little sister's friend Harry had big, big blue eyes and pretty golden curls like a baby angel, but oh dear, he was quite naughty all the same.

Now one day, when my little sister went round to play with Harry she

found him looking very smart indeed.
He was wearing real big boy's
trousers. Real ones, with real
big boy's buttons
and real big boy's
braces.   Red
braces like a very
big boy! Wasn't
he smart?

'Look,' said Bad
Harry, 'look at my
big boy's trousers.'

'Smart,' said my
naughty little sister, 'smart boy.'

'I'm going to have a real boy's
haircut too,' said Bad Harry. 'Today.

562

Not Mummy with scissors any more; but a real boy's haircut in a real barber's shop!'

My word, he was a proud boy!

My little sister was *so* surprised, and Bad Harry was so pleased to see how surprised she was.

'I'll be a big boy then,' he said.

Then Harry's mother, who was a kind lady and liked my little sister very much, said that if she was a good girl she could come to the barber's and see Harry have his hair cut.

My little sister was so excited that she ran straight back home at once to tell our mother all about Harry's big boy's trousers and Harry's real boy's haircut. 'Can I go too, can I go too?' she asked our mother.

Our mother said, 'Yes, you may go, only hold very tight to Harry's mother's hand when you cross the High Street,' and my little sister promised that she would hold very tight indeed.

So off they went to the barber's to get Harry a Real Boy's Haircut.

My little sister had never been in a barber's shop before and she stared and stared. Bad Harry had never been in a barber's shop before either, but he didn't stare, he pretended that he knew all about it, he picked up one of the barber's books and pretended to look at the pictures in it, but he peeped all the time at the barber's shop.

There were three haircut-men in the barber's shop, and they all had white coats and they all had black combs sticking out of their pockets.

There were three white wash-basins with shiny taps and looking-glasses, and three very funny chairs. In the three funny chairs were three men all having something done to them by the three haircut-men.

One man was having his hair cut with scissors, and one man was having his neck clipped with clippers, and one man had a soapy white face and *he* was being shaved!

And there were bottles and bottles, and brushes and brushes, and towels and towels, and pretty pictures with writing on them, and all sorts of things to see! My little sister looked and Bad Harry peeped until it was Harry's turn to have his hair cut.

When it was Harry's turn one of the haircut-men fetched a special high-chair for Harry to sit in, because the grown-up chairs were all too big.

Harry sat in the special chair and then the haircut-man got a big blue sheet and wrapped it round Harry and tucked it in at the neck. 'You don't want any tickly old hairs going down there,' the haircut-man said.

Then the haircut man took his sharp shiny scissors and began to cut and cut. And down fell a golden curl and 'Gone!' said my little sister, and down fell another golden curl and 'Gone!' said my little sister again, and she said, 'Gone!' 'Gone!' 'Gone!' all the time until Harry's curls had quite gone away. Then she said, 'All gone now!'

When the haircut-man had finished cutting he took a bottle with a squeezer-thing and he squirted some

nice smelly stuff all over Harry's head,
and made Harry laugh, and my little
sister laughed as well.

Then the haircut man took the big
black comb, and he made a Big Boy's
Parting on Harry's head, and he
combed Harry's hair back into a real

boy's haircut and then Bad Harry climbed down from the high-chair so that my little sister could really look at him.

And then my little sister *did* stare. Bad Harry's mother stared too . . .

For there was that bad boy Harry, with his real boy's trousers and his real boy's braces, with a real boy's haircut, smiling and smiling, and looking very pleased.

'No curls now,' said Bad Harry. 'Not any more.'

'No curls,' said my

naughty little sister.

'No,' Bad Harry's mother said, 'and oh dear, you don't even *look* good any more.'

Then my little sister laughed and laughed.

'Bad Harry!' she said. 'Bad Harry. All bad now – like me!'

9. My Naughty Little Sister shows off

Do you like climbing? My naughty little sister used to like climbing very much indeed. She climbed up fences and on chairs and down ditches and round railings, and my mother used to say, 'One day that child will fall and hurt herself.'

But our father said, 'She will be all right if she is careful.'

And my little sister *was* careful. She didn't want to hurt herself. She climbed on *easy things*, and when she knew she had gone far enough, she always came down again, slowly, slowly, carefully, carefully – one foot down – the other foot down – like that.

My little sister was so careful about climbing that our father nailed a piece of wood on to our front gate, so that she would have something to stand on when she wanted to look over it. There was a tree by the gate, and Father put an iron handle on the tree to help her to hold on tight. Wasn't he a kind daddy?

Well now, one day my naughty little sister went down to the front gate because she thought it would be nice to see all the people going by.

She climbed up carefully, carefully, like a good girl, and she held on to the iron handle, and she watched all the people going down the street.

First the postman came along. He said, 'Hello, Monkey,' and that made her laugh. She said, 'Hello, postman, have you any letters for this house?' and the postman said, 'Not today I'm afraid, Monkey.'

My little sister laughed again because the postman called her 'Monkey', but she remembered to hold on tight.

Then Mr Cocoa Jones went by on his bicycle. Mr Cocoa said, 'Don't fall,' and he ling-alinged his bicycle bell at her. 'Be very careful,' said Mr Cocoa Jones, and 'ling-aling', said Mr Cocoa Jones's bell.

My naughty little sister said, 'I won't fall. I won't fall, Mr Cocoa. I'm sensible,' and Mr Cocoa ling-a-linged his bell again and called 'Good-bye'.

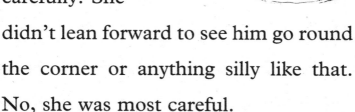

My naughty little sister waved to Mr Cocoa. She waved very carefully. She didn't lean forward to see him go round the corner or anything silly like that. No, she was most careful.

She was careful when the nice baker came with the bread. She climbed down, carefully, carefully and let him in.

She was careful when cars went by. She held tight and stood very still. She saw a steam-roller and a rag-a'-bone man, and she held very tight indeed.

Then my naughty little sister saw her friend, Bad Harry, coming down the road, and she forgot to be sensible. She began to show off.

My little sister shouted, 'Harry, Harry, look at me. I'm on the gate, Harry.'

Bad Harry did look at her, because she called in such a loud voice, 'Look at me!' like that.

Then my silly little sister stood on one leg only – just because she wanted Bad Harry to think she was a clever girl.

That made Bad Harry laugh, so my little sister showed off again. She

stood on the other leg only, and then –
*she let go of the tree and waved
her arms.*

And then – she fell right off the
gate. Bump! She fell down and
bumped her head.

Oh dear! Her head *did* hurt, and
my poor little sister cried and cried.
Bad Harry cried too, and my mother
came hurrying out of the house to see
what had happened.

Our dear mother said, 'Don't cry,
don't cry, baby,' in a kind, kind voice.
'Don't cry, baby dear,' she said, and
she picked my little sister up and took
her indoors and Bad Harry followed

them. They were still crying and crying.

They cried so much that my mother gave them each a sugar lump to suck. Then they stopped crying because they found that they couldn't cry and suck at the same time.

Then our mother looked at my little sister's poor head. 'What a nasty bruise,' our mother said. 'I think I had better put something on it for you, and you must be a good brave girl while I do it.'

My little sister was a good brave girl, too. She held Bad Harry's hand very tight, and she shut her eyes while

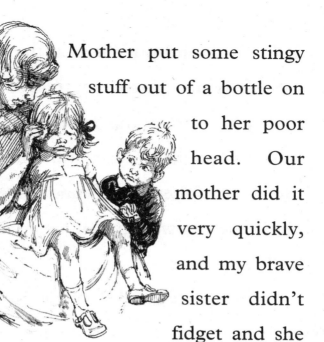

Mother put some stingy stuff out of a bottle on to her poor head. Our mother did it very quickly, and my brave sister didn't fidget and she didn't cry. Wasn't she good?

When our mother had finished she gave my little sister and her friend, Bad Harry, an apple each and they went into the garden to play.

They had a lovely time playing in the garden. First they picked dandelions and put them in the water-tub for boats. Then they played hide-and-seek among the cabbages. Then they made a little house underneath the apple-tree. Then they found some blue chalk and drew funny old men on the tool-shed door.

And my little sister forgot all about her poor head.

When our father came home and saw my naughty little sister playing in the garden he said, 'Hello, old lady, have you been in the wars?' and my little sister was surprised because she had forgotten all about falling off the gate. Father said, 'You have got a nasty lump on top!'

So my little sister thought she would go indoors and look at her nasty lump. She climbed up on to a chair to look at herself in the mirror on the kitchen wall, and she saw that there was a big bump on her forehead. It was all yellowy-greeny.

Our mother said, 'Climbing again! I should think you would have had enough climbing for one day!'

My little sister looked at her big bump in the mirror, and then she climbed down from the chair, carefully, carefully.

She climbed down very carefully

indeed, and do you know what she said? She said, 'I like climbing very much, but I don't like falling down. And I *certainly* don't like nasty bumps on my head. So I don't think I will be a showing-off girl any more.'

10. My Naughty Little Sister and the solid silver watch

A long time ago, when I was a little girl and my naughty little sister was very small, we had a dear old grandfather. Our dear old grandfather lived very near to us, and sometimes he came to our house, and sometimes we went to visit him.

When our grandfather came to see us, he wore very beautiful black clothes and a very smart black hat, and my little sister would say, 'Smart Grandad,' because he looked so nice.

Our grandfather told my little sister

that these smart clothes were his Sunday Blacks. He said he wore his Sunday Blacks when he went to church and when he went visiting, because they were his best clothes.

When our grandfather came to our house in his smart Sunday Blacks, he always sat down very carefully. He would put a big white handkerchief on his knees, and then lift my little sister up and let her sit on the big white handkerchief. But my little sister had to hold her legs out very carefully so that she wouldn't brush her dusty shoes on our grandfather's best Sunday Black trousers.

But when we went to see our grandfather in his house, he didn't wear his Sunday Blacks at all. He wore nice brown velvety trousers, with straps under his knees, and a soft furry waistcoat. He had a lovely red and white handkerchief too, but he didn't put that on his knees for my little sister to sit on.

Oh no. Grandfather didn't mind my little sister's dirty shoes when he was wearing his velvety trousers. He would let her climb up on to his lap all on her own and didn't mind how dirty her shoes were.

When my little sister sat on our

grandfather's lap, she always rubbed her face against his waistcoat. If she rubbed her face against his Sunday Black waistcoat, she rubbed it very, very carefully. But when we were at Grandfather's house she rubbed very hard against his soft furry one.

One day, when we were at our grandfather's house, and my naughty little sister was sitting on Grandfather's lap, she said a funny thing, she said:

'Grandad, I like your fur waistcoat better than your smart Sunday Black one. It smells tobacco-y. Your Sunday one smells mothball-y. I like tobacco better than mothball I think.'

Our grandfather laughed a lot and said he liked tobacco better than mothball too.

Then my little sister said, 'Your Sunday waistcoat and your furry waistcoat both talk *nick-nock, nick-nock*. Why do they both talk *nick-nock*, Grandad?'

Our grandfather didn't know what she meant about *nick-nock*, so he looked at my little sister very hard. Then he smiled and said, 'Of course, duckie, you mean my watch!'

Then our grandfather showed my little sister a thin leather strap that was on his waistcoat button and he said,

'Pull the strap, and you'll see who it is that says *nick-nock* – it isn't my waistcoat that says it at all.'

So my funny little sister pulled the thin leather strap. She pulled very slowly, and very carefully, because she was a little bit frightened, but when she had pulled enough out came a round silver box-thing with a round silver lid on it.

Our grandfather opened the round silver lid and there was a face just like the face on all the clocks everywhere.

'That's my watch,' our grandfather told my little sister. 'That is my solid silver watch. My old father had it once, and one day your father will have it. It is a very nice watch,' our grandfather said, 'it is *solid* silver.'

My little sister held the solid silver watch very carefully and looked at its round white face and the black clockhands and the little round silver lid. Then my little sister put the solid silver watch against her ear and listened to it saying *nick-nock, nick-nock, nick-nock,* over and over again.

My little sister liked the watch so much that she held it all the time. Very carefully, like a good child, my little sister held the solid silver watch.

When it was time to go, our mother

said, 'You must give the watch back to
Grandad now, so that he can put it in

his pocket again,' and my naughty little sister began to look cross, because she *did* like the solid silver watch so much.

But our grandfather said, 'I will let you put him back to bed for me, duckie, then he will be quite safe until you see me again.'

So then my little sister stopped being a cross girl and put the solid silver watch back into our grandfather's pocket her own self.

She said, 'I don't think I should like to go to bed in your pocket, Grandad. But the solid silver watch does. He still says *nick-nock*, doesn't he?'

After that my naughty little sister always asked to see the solid silver watch when she was with our grandfather, and he always let her hold it and listen to it say *nick-nock*.

And do you know, one evening, when our father and mother had to go out, our dear old grandfather came to look after us, and because my little sister was such a good girl, and went to bed so quietly, and said her prayers so nicely, our grandfather put his solid silver watch under her pillow, so that she could hear it say *nick-nock nick-nock* until she fell asleep.

11. Mrs Cocoa's white visitor

One cold and frosty morning, when I was a little girl and my sister was a very little girl, our mother and Mrs Jones next door and all the ladies living near us did lots and lots of washing and pegged it out on their clothes-lines.

There was a lot of hard cold snow on the ground, and there was a cold wind blowing, and my little sister was kneeling by the kitchen window watching Mother's washing and Mrs Cocoa Jones's washing and all

the other ladies' washing blowing
and blowing, and she laughed and
laughed.

My sister was laughing because all
the washing was frozen. The wind had
blown it, and the frost had frozen it
into funny shapes. Mother's big sheets

had gone all pointy-looking, and the tea-towels were sticking right up in the air. Mr Jones's woollies and socks looked hard and cold with icy teardrops hanging on them.

As for my sister's own little knickers and petticoats, the wind had blown them out into funny little balloons, and the frost had frozen them into funny little balloons, and they bobbed and bobbed on the line.

No wonder my sister laughed at the washing.

The wind blew 'whoo-oo' – like that – and the washing went 'snap-crack' on the line because it was so frozen.

'Will they stay like that now?' my sister said. 'Will they always be hard and funny-looking?'

'Oh no,' Mother told her. 'The sun will thaw them, and the wind will blow the water out of the clothes, and they will be quite soft again.'

'I am very glad about that,' said my little sister. 'I shouldn't like balloony knickers very much!'

And she went back to the window to see if the wind had blown them soft yet. She looked at all the whiteness. The cold snow white and the cold sheet white. All cold and white.

Then suddenly my sister shouted

and shouted, 'Mother, look, look!' she said. 'A big white washing-thing fell out of the sky on to Mrs Cocoa's garden.'

Mother said, 'Good gracious,' and looked out of the window, but she couldn't see anything.

But my sister jumped and jumped on the window-seat she was so excited. 'It fell down, it fell down,' she said, and jumped and jumped.

'You'll fall down too, if you aren't careful,' our mother said.

'I saw it, I saw it,' said my naughty little sister in a cross voice because she thought my mother wasn't being interested. 'It was all white and sheety-looking.'

And she might have shown off and been very cross indeed, only just then we heard Mrs Cocoa calling and calling, and we all ran out into the cold and frosty garden without thinking about our coats even, for dear Mrs Cocoa was saying, 'Help, help!'

Oh yes. My little sister *had* seen something come out of the sky; but it wasn't washing, and I don't think it really fell, but it must have looked as if it did.

It was a great white bird. A great white bird, with a long long neck and a black and yellow beak. It had come down into Mrs Cocoa Jones's garden, and Mrs Cocoa was saying, 'Help, help.'

Poor Mrs Cocoa had been hanging out some sheets when the bird came down and it had given her a fright. That was why she had shouted like that.

'Why,' said Mother, 'it's a swan!'

And so it was. My sister knew swans; she had seen them in the park. Sometimes we had gone to take bread to them. So now she had a good idea. She said, 'Give him some bread, Mrs Cocoa.'

Mrs Cocoa stopped being frightened. She said, 'What a clever girl you are,' and she hurried indoors to find a big piece of bread for the swan.

That was just what the swan wanted. He turned down his bendy head, and snapped with his black and yellow beak, and he swallowed up the piece of bread at once.

Our mother told us to go indoors and put our coats on, and while we did this, she found some stale bread for us to give the swan.

When Mrs Jones saw the swan eating bread in her snowy garden she became quite pleased and smiley, because swans don't often come into gardens, and some of the ladies from the other houses were beginning to look over their fences and say, 'Fancy that!' and 'Look – in Mrs Jones's garden – there's a swan!' It made dear Mrs Cocoa quite famous. It made my sister feel famous too because she had seen the swan first!

That swan was a very greedy bird. It wanted more and more to eat. Mrs Cocoa was glad when Mr Cocoa Jones came home on his bicycle for his dinner.

When Mr Cocoa saw the swan he said, 'That old fellow comes from the park. He's been out before.'

Then he said that the pond in the park was frozen hard, and he expected the swan had decided to fly away and look for a warmer place. Mr Cocoa said the swan couldn't fly far though, because the park swans had had something done to their wings to stop them going too far and becoming nuisances.

'It's a wonder it got as far as this,' Mr Jones said.

My sister asked Mr Cocoa if he was going to keep the swan now, but Mr Cocoa Jones was very shocked. 'Good gracious, no,' he said. 'That bird is *Crown Property*.'

He said that a man with a funny name would have to come and collect it.

My sister told me what Mr Jones

said, and she told me the man's funny name, she said, 'Mr Jones says he is going to stop at the Speeseeay man's house on his way back to work and ask him to fetch the swan.'

And she talked about the swan and the Speeseeay man all the time she was eating her dinner.

Presently two men came to Mrs Cocoa's house with a little green van. They said they knew the swan very well indeed; they said he was a 'bit of a rover'.

Then they asked everyone to go indoors, so that the swan wouldn't be upset. They said they knew just how to deal with him.

We went indoors, but we watched from a bedroom window where the swan could not see us. We saw the Speeseeay man and his friend throw some special food to the swan that it seemed to like very much. They kept throwing it, and walking backwards, and the swan followed, eating, right out of Mrs Cocoa's back gate.

They threw more food and more food until they came to the van, and it followed the food up to the van, and up a little plank into the back of the van, and when it was inside, and they had made it comfortable, the Speeseeay man and his friend drove the swan back to the park.

And it was just as well, because next day the snow and ice began to melt away, and the pond turned to water again.

After that, when my sister saw the little green van with RSPCA on it running about the town she always waved to it, and said, 'There goes the Speeseeay man!'

My Naughty Little Sister and Bad Harry

Contents

1. My Naughty Little Sister and Bad Harry

Once upon a time – a long time ago – when I was a little girl, I had a sister who was littler than me. Now although my sister was sometimes very naughty she had a lot of friends. Some of her friends were grown-up people but some were quite young. Her favourite child-friend was a little boy called Harry. He often made my sister cross so she called him Bad Harry.

Bad Harry lived quite near to us. There were no roads to cross to get to his house, and he and my sister often went round to visit each other without any grown-up person having to take them.

One day, when my naughty little sister went round to Bad Harry's house it was his mother's washing day. Bad Harry was very pleased to see her; he didn't like it when his mother was doing washing.

'Have you come to play?' he asked.

Now Harry's mother didn't like naughty children running about in her house while she was doing the washing, so she said, 'You'll have to play in the garden then. You know what you two are like when there's

616

water about!'

Harry said he didn't mind that. There was a lovely game they could play in the garden. They could play *Islands*.

There was a big heap of sand at the bottom of the garden that Harry's father was going to make a path with one day. Harry said, 'We'll pretend that sand is an island in the river, like the one we go to on the ferry-boat sometimes.'

My sister said, 'Yes. We will go and live on it. We will say that all the garden is the river.'

So off they went.

They had a good game pretending
to live on the island. They filled
Harry's toy truck with sand and ran it
up and down the heap and tipped the
sand over the island's side until it
became quite flat.

Then they dug holes in the sand and stuck sticks in them and said they were planting trees.

Later on Harry went to find some more sticks and while he was gone my sister made sand-pies for their pretending dinner. My little sister made them in a flower-pot and tipped them out very carefully. They did look nice.

'Dinner time, Harry,' she said.

But instead of pretending to eat a sand pie, that bad Bad Harry knocked all the pies over with a stick.

He said, 'Now you will have to make some more.'

He thought that was a funny thing to do. But my sister didn't think so.

My naughty little sister was very, very cross with Bad Harry when he knocked her pies over. She screamed and shouted and said, 'Get off my island, bad, Bad Harry,' and she pushed him and he fell on to the garden.

When Harry fell my sister stopped being cross. She laughed instead. 'Now you're all wet in the river,' she said.

But Bad Harry didn't laugh. He was very angry.

'I'm not wet. I'm not wet,' he

shouted, and he began to jump up and down. 'You pushed me. You pushed me,' Harry said.

'You broke my pies,' shouted my sister, 'Bad old Harry,' and *she* jumped up and down too.

Bad Harry was just going to shout again when he saw something and had an idea: he saw his mother's washing-basket.

Harry's mother had filled the washing-line with sheets and she'd left the other wet things in a basket on the path so that she could hang them up when the sheets were dry.

'I've got a boat,' Harry said.

He went up to the basket with the wet things in it.

'Look,' he said. 'It's a boat!' And he began to push it along the path.

My sister forgot about being cross with Harry because she liked his idea so much. She went to help him push.

'We've got a boat,' she said.

They pushed their boat round and round the island, and they were just talking about giving each other rides in it, on top of the wet washing, and my sister was just shouting again because she wanted to be first, when Harry's mother came out.

'You are naughty children,' Harry's

mother said. 'If I hadn't caught you in time you would have got all my washing dirty. What will you do next?'

'We were playing Islands,' Bad Harry said.

'Well, you are not going to play Islands any more,' said Harry's mother. 'You will come indoors with me where I can keep an eye on you!'

'Now,' she said. 'You can each sit on a chair while I wash the kitchen floor.'

She lifted Bad Harry on to one chair, and my naughty little sister on to another chair, and she said, 'Don't you *dare* get off!'

And they *didn't* dare get off.

Harry's mother looked too cross. They didn't even talk – they were so busy watching her washing the floor.

First she used the mop on one corner. Then she picked up the chair with Bad Harry on it and put it on the wet place.

'There!' she said.

Then she washed the floor in another corner. She picked up the chair with my naughty little sister on it and put it on that wet place.

'There!' she said. 'Now don't get down till the floor is dry!'

She said, 'Curl your feet up and keep them out of the wet.'

And Bad Harry curled his feet, and my little sister curled her feet, and Bad Harry's mother laughed and said, 'Right, here I go!'

And she mopped all the floor that was left. She did it very, very quickly.

My little sister quite enjoyed watching Harry's mother mop the floor. She liked to see the mop going round and round and all the soap bubbles going round and round too. She liked to see it going backwards and forwards wiping up the bubbles. Every time the bubbles were wiped up she shouted, 'Gone away!' Our mother didn't clean *her* floor like that – so it was very interesting.

Bad Harry didn't shout though. He went very still and very quiet. He was thinking.

When Harry's mother was finished, she said, '*Well*, you *have* been good children. I'll just put some newspaper over the floor and you can get down.'

So she put newspaper all over the floor, and my little sister got down off her chair.

'Let's go and find a chocolate biscuit,' Harry's kind mother said.

My little sister smiled because she liked chocolate biscuits, but Bad Harry didn't smile. He didn't get down from his chair. He was still thinking.

He was pretending. All the time he had been on the chair he had been playing Islands. He had been pretending that the chair was an island and the wet floor was a river.

'Come on, Harry,' my naughty little sister said. 'Come and get your biscuit.'

'I can't. I'll fall in the river,' said Harry. 'I can't swim yet.'

My little sister knew at once that Harry had been playing. She looked at the wet floor with the paper all over it, then she pulled the paper across the floor and laid it in a line from Harry's chair to the door. 'Come over the bridge,' she said.

And that's what he did. And after that they made up all sorts of games with newspapers on the floor.

2. The icy cold tortoise

Long ago, when I was a little girl and had a little sister, we lived next door to a kind lady called Mrs Jones. My sister used to call this lady Mrs Cocoa sometimes.

If my mother had to go out and couldn't take my little sister this kind next-door lady used to mind her. My sister was always glad to be minded by dear Mrs Jones and Mrs Cocoa Jones was always glad to mind my little sister. They enjoyed minding days very much.

Well now, one cold blowy day when the wind was pulling all the old leaves off the trees to make room for the new baby ones to grow, our mother asked Mrs Cocoa Jones to mind my sister while she went shopping.

Mrs Cocoa and my sister had a lovely time. They swept up all the leaves from Mr Jones's nice tidy paths and put them into a heap for him to burn. They went indoors and laid Mr Jones's tea, and they were just going to sit down by the fire to have a rest when they heard Mr Cocoa coming down the back path.

Mr Cocoa came down the path

pushing his bicycle with one hand and holding a very strange-looking wooden box with holes in it in the other hand.

When Mr Jones saw my little sister peeping at him out of his kitchen window he smiled and smiled. 'Hello, Mrs Pickle,' he said. 'What are you doing here, then?'

'I'm being minded,' said my little sister. Then, because she was an inquisitive child she said, 'What have you got in that box, Mr Cocoa?'

'Just wait a minute, and I'll show you,' Mr Cocoa said, and he went off to put his bicycle in the shed.

'I wonder what's in that box, Mrs Cocoa?' said my inquisitive little sister.

'It's a very funny box – it's got holes in it.'

'Ah,' said Mrs Cocoa, 'just you wait and see!'

When kind Mr Cocoa came in and saw my impatient little sister he was so good he didn't even stop to take off his coat. He opened the box at *once* – and he showed my sister an icy-cold tortoise, lying fast asleep under a lot of hay.

Have you ever seen a tortoise? My little sister hadn't.

Tortoises are very strange animals. They have hard round shells and long crinkly necks and little beaky noses.

They have tiny black eyes and four scratchy-looking claws.

But when they are asleep you can't see their heads or their claws; they are tucked away under their shells. They just look like cold round stones.

My little sister thought the tortoise was a stone at first. She touched it, and it was icy-cold. 'What is it?' she said. 'What is this stone-thing?'

Mr Cocoa picked the tortoise up and showed her where the little claws were tucked away, and the beaky little shut-eyed face under the shell.

'It's a tortoise,' Mr Cocoa said.

'He's having his winter sleep now,'

said Mrs Cocoa.

Mr Jones told my sister that one of the men who worked with him had given him the tortoise, because he was going away and wouldn't have anywhere to keep it in his new home.

'I shall put him away in the cupboard under the stairs now,' he said. 'He will sleep there all the winter and wake up again when the warm days come.'

Just as Mr Cocoa said this, the tortoise opened its little beady black eyes and looked at my sister. Then it closed them and went to sleep again. So Mr Cocoa put it away in its box right at the back of the cupboard under the stairs.

'That's a funny animal,' my naughty little sister said.

After that, she talked and talked about the tortoise. She kept saying, 'When will it wake up? – When will it wake up?' But it didn't so she got tired of asking. By the time Christmas came she had almost forgotten it. And when the snow fell she quite forgot it.

And when spring came and the birds began to sing again, and she went in one day to have her morning cocoa with her next-door friend, Mrs Jones had forgotten it too!

They were just drinking their cocoa and Mrs Jones was telling my naughty little sister about some of the things she had done when she was a little girl when they heard:

Thump! Thump! Bang! Bang!

'Oh dear,' said Mrs Cocoa. 'There's someone at the front door!' And she went to look. But there wasn't.

Thump! Thump!

'It must be the back door,' said Mrs Cocoa Jones, and she went to look but it wasn't!

Bang! Bang!

'What can it be?' asked Mrs Jones.

Now, my clever little sister had been

listening hard. 'It's in the under-the-stairs place, Mrs Cocoa,' she said. 'Listen.'

Thump! Thump! Bang! Bang!

'Oh goodness,' said Mrs Cocoa. But she was a very brave lady. She opened the door of the cupboard and looked and my little sister looked too.

And Mrs Cocoa stared and my little sister stared.

There was the tortoise's wooden box, shaking and bumping because the cross tortoise inside had woken up and was banging to be let out.

'Goodness me,' said Mrs Cocoa. 'That tortoise has woken up!'

'Goodness me,' said my funny sister. 'That tortoise has woken up!'

And Mrs Cocoa looked hard at my sister and my sister looked hard at her.

'I shall have to see to it,' Mrs Cocoa said, and she picked up the bumping box and carried it into her kitchen and put the box on the table. Then she lifted my sister up to the chair so she could watch.

Mrs Cocoa lifted the lid off the box, and there was that wide-awake tortoise. His head was waggle-waggling and his claws scratch-scratching to get out.

'I used to have a tortoise when I

was a girl,' Mrs Cocoa said, 'so I know just what to do!'

And do you know what she did? She put some warm water into a bowl, and she put the tortoise in the warm water. Then she took it out and dried it very, very carefully on an old soft towel.

Then Mrs Cocoa put the clean fresh tortoise on the table, and said, 'Just mind it while I go and get it something to eat, there's a good child. Just put your hand gently on his back and he will stay quite still.'

My little sister did keep her hand on the tortoise's back and he was quite still until Mrs Cocoa came back with a cabbage leaf.

'Look,' my naughty little sister said, 'look at his waggly head, Mrs Jones.'

And she put her face right down so she could see his little black eyes. 'Hello, Mister Tortoise,' she said.

And the tortoise made a funny noise at her. It said, 'His-ss-SS.'

My poor sister was surprised! She didn't like that noise very much. But Mrs Cocoa said the tortoise had only said, 'His-ss-SS' because it was hungry and not because it was cross. Mrs Cocoa said tortoises are nice friendly things so long as you let them go their own way.

And because my little sister had minded the tortoise for her she let her give him the cabbage leaf.

At first he only looked at it, and pushed it about with his beaky head, but at last he bit a big piece out of it.

'There!' Mrs Jones said. 'That's the first thing he's tasted since last summer!'

Just fancy that!

Mr Cocoa made the tortoise a little home in his rockery where it could sleep, and it could walk around among the stones or hide among the rockery flowers if it wanted to.

Sometimes it used to eat the flowers, and make Mr Cocoa cross.

That tortoise lived with the Cocoa Joneses for many, many years. It slept under the stairs in the winter and walked about the rockery in summer. It was still there when my sister was a grown-up lady.

Mr and Mrs Cocoa called it Henry, but of course when my sister was little she always called it Henry Cocoa Jones.

3. My Naughty Little Sister and Bad Harry at the library

Nowadays libraries are very nice places where there are plenty of picture-books for children to look at, and a very nice lady who will let you take some home to read so long as you promise not to tear them or scribble in them.

When I was a little girl we had a library in the town where we lived. Our mother used to go there once a week to get a book to read, and when I was old enough I used to go with her to get a book for myself.

Our library wasn't as nice as the one nearest to your house. There wasn't a special children's part. The children's books were in a corner among the grown-up books, and all the books had dark brown library-covers — no nice bright picture-covers. You had to look inside them to find out what the stories were about.

Still, when I did look, I found some very good stories just as you do nowadays.

But we didn't have very nice people to give out the books.

There was a cross old man with glasses who didn't like children very much. When we brought our book back he would look through it very carefully to make sure we hadn't messed it up and grumble if he found a spot or a tear – even if it was nothing to do with us.

And there was a lady who used to say, 'Sh-sh-sh' all the time, and come and grumble if you held one book while you were looking at another one. She would say, 'All books to be returned to the shelves immediately.'

My little sister went to the library with us once, but she said she wouldn't come any more because she didn't like the shushy lady and the glasses man.

So after that Mrs Cocoa Jones minded her on library days.

So, you can imagine how surprised we were one day when she said, 'I want to go to the library.'

Our mother said, 'But you don't like the library. You're always saying how nasty it is there.'

But my little sister said, 'Yes, I do. I do like it *now*.'

She said, 'I don't want to go with you though, I want to go with Bad Harry's mother.'

What a surprise!

Our mother said, 'I don't suppose Harry's mother wants to take *you*. It must be hard enough for her with Harry.'

But, do you know, Harry's mother *did* want to take my sister. Bad Harry's mother said, '*Please* let her come with us. Harry has been worrying and worrying to ask you.'

So my mother said my little sister could go to the library with Bad Harry and his mother, but she said she thought she had better come along too.

'I don't trust those two bad children when they're together,' our mother said.

All the way to the library those naughty children walked in front of their mothers whispering and giggling together, and our mother said, 'I just hope they won't get up to mischief.'

But Harry's mother said, 'Oh no! *Harry is always as quiet as a mouse in the library.*'

Bad Harry – quiet as a mouse! Fancy that.

But so he was. And so was my sister. They were both as quiet as two mice.

When they got to the library, the man with glasses wasn't cross, he said, 'Hello, sonny,' to Bad Harry and that was a surprise. (But of course at that time Harry still looked good.)

And then the shushing lady came

along. She smiled at Harry, and Harry smiled at her, and the lady looked at my naughty little sister and said, 'We don't mind good children like Harry coming here!'

My little sister was very surprised, and so was my mother, but Harry's mother said, 'Harry is always good in the library. He goes and sits in the little book-room in the corner, and he doesn't make a sound until I'm ready to go!'

Harry's mother said, 'He looks at the books on the table and he is as good as gold.'

Of course our mother was worried because she thought my sister couldn't be like that, but she let my sister go with Harry while she went to find herself a new book to read.

And, do you know, all the time our mother and Harry's mother were choosing books those children were quiet as mice.

And when our mother and Harry's mother were ready to go, there they were sitting good as gold, looking at a book in the little book-room.

When our mother got home she said, 'I would never have believed it. Those children were like *angels*!'

So after that my naughty little sister often went to the library with

Bad Harry and his mother. And they were always quiet as mice.

Then one day Bad Harry's mother found out why.

One day when they were in the library she found a book very quickly, and, when she went along to the little book-room she had a great surprise. She couldn't see them anywhere!

Then she looked again, and there they were – under the book-table.

They were lying very still on their tummies, staring at something, and, as Harry's mother bent down to see what they were doing, a tiny mouse ran over the floor and into a hole in the wall!

You see, the very first time Harry had visited the library, he had seen that little mouse, and afterwards he always looked out for it.

He used to take things for it to eat sometimes: pieces of cheese and bacon-rind. The mouse had been Bad Harry's secret friend, and now it was my sister's secret friend too.

Harry's mother told our mother all about those funny children and the library mouse. She said, 'I suppose I ought to tell the librarian.'

But our mother said, 'I don't see why. That old man is always nibbling biscuits. He keeps them under the counter. He just encourages mice.'

I hadn't known about the biscuit nibbling, but the next time I went to get a book I peeped, and Mother was right. There was a bag of biscuits under the cross man's counter and piles of biscuit crumbs!

No wonder there was a library

mouse. And no
wonder it made
friends with
Bad Harry. 
The cheese and bacon
bits must have been a great change
from biscuit crumbs, mustn't they?

4. Grandad's special holly

In the long time ago when I was a little girl with a naughty little sister, we had a dear old grandad who had two gardens. He had a pretty little garden round his house with flowers and apples in it, and a big garden near the park for vegetables. The garden near the park was called an allotment. It had a tall hedge at the bottom of it, and in this tall hedge was a big tree with green-and-white leaves. It was a very, very prickly tree.

We used to go and see Grandad

when he was working on his allotment. We used to take him something to drink because he said digging made him thirsty. In summer he had a jug of cold tea and in winter he had a jug of hot cocoa. In summer he would sit on his wheelbarrow and drink his tea and talk to us and in the wintertime we used to go into his allotment shed and warm our hands by the oil-stove while he drank his cocoa.

One day, when Grandad was drinking cold tea and the sun was shining, my little sister said, 'I don't like your prickly tree very much, Grandad. It prickled my fingers.'

Grandad said, 'That's a very special tree, that is. That's a variegated holly-tree. You don't see trees like that every day.' He said it in a very proud way.

He said, 'When Christmas-time comes it will be full of red berries.'

Then he told us that every Christmas Eve he would bring a ladder and climb up the holly-tree and cut off some of its beautiful green-and-white branches with the red berries. He would put the cut holly into his wheelbarrow and take it down to the Church.

Every Christmas Eve afternoon he

took his holly to the Church so the church-ladies could hang it up on the walls and make them look nice for Christmas.

Grandad said, 'When I go to Church on Christmas Morning, I like to look up and see the greenery. I can always pick out my holly, it's special.'

When my little sister told our father about the holly he said he remembered how when he was a little boy he used to go with Grandad to take the Church-holly on Christmas Eve. He said he could still remember going through the town with all the people pointing and saying, 'Look at the lovely holly!'

My little sister was pleased to hear about our father being a little boy and going to the Church with Grandad and the holly, and the next time we went to the allotment she told Grandad *she* would like to go with him on Christmas Eve.

And Grandad said well, if Mother didn't mind he'd be very pleased to take her when Christmas Eve came.

Our mother said she didn't mind a bit, because she knew Grandad would take great care of my sister. She said when Christmas Eve came if she still wanted to go with Grandad it would be quite all right.

'Christmas Eve is a long way off,' our mother said. 'You may change your mind by then.'

But my naughty little sister *didn't* change her mind. Every time she saw Grandad she said, 'How are the hollyberries?' And when he showed her how they were growing and how red they were getting she got very impatient.

She kept saying, 'Will it soon be Christmas?' She was so afraid our dear old grandad would forget and take the holly without her.

But he didn't. On the very next Christmas Eve, just after we'd eaten our dinner there was a loud knock on the front-door, and when Mother opened it – there was Grandad smiling and smiling and outside the gate was his great big wheelbarrow piled high with the lovely green-and-white and red-berried holly.

Some of the people in the road were looking out of their windows, and while our mother was putting my sister's warm coat on and tying the red woolly scarf round her neck, a lady came to our door and asked if Grandad would sell her some holly.

Grandad said, 'No, I'm very sorry, all this is for the Church.' But he gave the lady a little piece for her Christmas pudding and the lady was very glad to have it. My little sister said the lady's pudding would look very grand with special holly on it, and the lady said she was sure it would.

Now it was a long walk to the Church, so our grandad said my little sister had better ride on the wheelbarrow. He had put some sacks in front of the barrow over the prickly leaves, and my little sister climbed on and sat down, and off they went.

My naughty little sister *did* enjoy that ride, even though the holly prickles poked through the sacks and

scratched her a little bit. It was just like Father had said. All the people stared and said, 'What lovely holly!' and smiled at my little sister with her holly-berry red scarf sitting in front of Grandad's wheelbarrow.

They had to go down the High Street where the shops were because the Church was there too, and a man who sold oranges gave my sister one. He said, 'Happy Christmas, ducks,' to her as she went by. Wasn't that nice of him? My sister thought it was and so did Grandad.

When they got to the Church the ladies all came out to look at

Grandad's big load of variegated holly.

Grandad said, 'Lift it carefully, we don't want the berries knocked off.'

While Grandad and some of the ladies were taking the branches inside, one of the ladies talked to my little sister. She said, 'Would you like to come and see the manger?'

My little sister knew about 'Way in a Manger' and about Baby Jesus being born at Christmas-time, so although she didn't know what the lady meant she said, 'Yes,' because she knew it would be something nice.

And so it was.

That kind lady took my little sister

into the cold grey church where a lot of people were making it look bright and Christmassy with holly and ivy and white flowers in pots. My naughty little sister wanted to stop and look at a man on a ladder who was handing up some Christmas-tree branches, but the lady said, 'Come on.'

Then she said, 'There! It's just finished. Isn't it pretty?'

And there, in a corner of the cold old church someone had built a wooden shed with a manger with straw in it inside. There was a statue of Mary and a statue of Joseph standing on each side of the manger, and on the straw inside it was a little stony Baby Jesus statue.

There was a picture of an ox and a donkey on the wall at the back of the shed, and round the shed doorway were pictures of angels.

My little sister said, 'My grandad's got a shed like that on his allotment. He's got a stove in it though.'

And she looked very hard at the Mary statue and the Joseph statue and the Baby Jesus statue.

The lady said, 'The Sunday School children always bring toys to Church on Christmas Day to send to the children in hospital. They leave them by the manger because that's where the shepherds put their presents.' The lady said that tomorrow morning there would be some shepherd statues by the manger too.

Then she said, 'You can stay and look if you like. I'll just go and help your grandaddy to break up some of the holly branches.'

So my naughty little sister stayed there, looking and looking. It was very cold in that big church. Mary looked cold and Joseph looked cold too. Very, very carefully my little sister leaned into the shed and touched the little Baby Jesus statue and he was cold as ice!

My naughty little sister stayed by
the manger for a little while longer and
then she went to find Grandad who
was ready to go home. There was lots

of room in the wheelbarrow now, and lots more things to see on the way home, but my little sister was very, very quiet.

And what do you think happened?

The next day, which was Christmas Day of course, when I went with the other Sunday School boys and girls to leave a present by the manger for the ill children, we saw a very strange thing.

There were Mary and Joseph. The Shepherds were there too. And there was the little Baby Jesus!

But the little Baby Jesus wasn't cold any more. He was wrapped up in my naughty little sister's red woolly scarf, and he had an orange beside him!

The Sunday School teacher said, 'Your funny little sister did that last night! Wasn't that sweet of her? She thought he was cold!'

5. Granny's wash-day

Long ago, when I was a little girl with a naughty little sister we had two grannies. We had a granny who lived near us and a granny in the country.

We could see our near-granny whenever we wanted to, but we only saw our country-granny when we could go and stay with her.

Our country-granny lived in a pretty house with roses all over it. It was a funny house. One of the funny things about it was that there were no taps in it at all.

There was a big pump in the back garden. This pump was on top of a deep well full of clear cold water. Our granny got all her water out of that well.

One time my naughty little sister went to stay with this granny and she liked it very much. There were five kind uncles living there too and they made a great fuss of my little sister.

But although these uncles were so kind they made such a lot of noise and needed such a lot of looking-after and ate such very big dinners that my little sister said, 'I shan't have any boys when I'm a lady.'

Every day our granny cooked big dinners for all the hungry uncles. Every day our hungry uncles ate all the big dinners up. On *Sunday* Granny cooked such a *big, big* dinner that my little sister said, 'Do the uncles eat more than ever because it's Sunday?'

'Oh, no, my dear,' our granny said. 'I always cook extra potatoes and extra cabbage for *bubble-and-squeak*. Tomorrow is wash-day,' Granny said. 'I don't have time for much cooking on wash-day.'

When Granny said 'bubble-and-squeak' my little sister laughed. She hadn't heard about bubble-and-squeak before. So she said it lots of times. She said, 'Bubble-and-squeak, bubble-and-squeak,' over and over again. It sounded so bubbly and so squeaky when she said it to herself that she could hardly stop laughing at all.

When my little sister *did* stop laughing she asked what 'bubble-and-squeak' was. But our granny said, 'Wait until tomorrow and then you can taste some.'

(Do you know what bubble-and-squeak is? If you don't you'll know at the end of the story.)

Well, next day was Monday and Monday was wash-day at our granny's house.

Our granny's wash-day was a very busy day. Everyone got up very, very early. Even my little sister. She heard all the people moving about and she got up to see what they were doing.

Our uncles carried lots of large pails out to the garden, and pumped up water and filled all the pails up to the top. Then those kind men carried all the heavy pails back to the house and left them by the back door. They wanted to help their mother so they fetched all the water for wash-day before they had their breakfasts.

When our uncles had gone off to work my little sister helped Granny too. She helped Granny collect all the dirty things that had to be washed.

My little sister liked helping to do this. It was great fun. Granny took all the sheets and pillow-cases off the beds and all the towels and our uncles' dirty shirts and things and she put them outside the bedroom doors. Then my little sister took all the sheets and pillow-cases and towels and all the other things from outside the bedroom doors and *she threw them all down the* stairs. And she wasn't being naughty.

She threw them down the stairs because Granny said it saved carrying them down.

It was very nice throwing the dirty things down the stairs and my little sister was sorry when there was nothing left to throw. But she was a good child. She went downstairs with Granny and helped her to carry the things out to the wash-house next to the back-door.

Do you know what a wash-house is? I will tell you what our granny's wash-house was like. It was a long room. In a corner there was a big copper for boiling the water. There was a fire burning under the copper to make the water hot. There was a big sink and lots of big baths full of cold water for rinsing the washing.

Granny had a big wringer for wringing the wet clothes in her wash-house. She had some clothes lines too. She had them hanging up in the wash-house in case it rained on wash-day.

A lady called Mrs Apple came to help Granny do her washing. She had a brown apron on with a big pocket in front of it, and this big pocket was full of pegs.

My little sister had never seen such a big wash-day before. She was so

interested she got in Granny's way. She got in Mrs Apple's way too. Mrs Apple dipped a funny little bag full of blue stuff into one of the baths full of water and made the water blue, and my naughty little sister liked it so much she splashed and dabbled in it and got herself wet.

Granny said, 'Oh dear, you're as bad as your mother used to be on wash-days when she was your age.'

My sister was surprised to hear that our mother had been a naughty little girl when she was little.

Kind Mrs Apple said, 'Ah, but your mummy was a good girl too. Now, see if you can be a good girl.' And she gave my little sister a basin full of warm water and let her wash her own cotton socks and handkerchiefs. Mrs Apple said, 'It will be a great help if you do those.'

So my little sister rubbed and rubbed and when they were as clean as they could be, kind Mrs Apple let her put them into the big copper for boiling.

She held my little sister up so that she could drop the socks and handkerchiefs in for herself. Then Mrs Apple put more wood on the copper fire and said, 'They will all cook nicely now.'

Then Mrs Apple washed and washed and our granny rinsed and rinsed. The wringer was turned and the water ran out of the clothes. The copper steamed and steamed and my little sister was so interested and got in the way so much that at last our granny said, 'I know what I will do with you. I will do the same thing I used to do to your mother and your uncles when they got in the way on wash-days.'

What do you think that was? It was something very nice. Our granny went to a shelf and took down a little chair-swing with strong ropes on it. Then she climbed up on a chair and my little sister saw that there were two big hooks in the wash-house roof. Granny put the ropes over the hooks. She tried the swing with her hands to make sure it was safe and strong and then she lifted my naughty little sister into the swing and gave it a big push.

My little sister had a lovely time swinging in the steamy splashy wash-house. Now she was not in the way at all and she could see everything that was happening.

Sometimes Granny gave her a little push. Sometimes Mrs Apple pushed. Sometimes my little sister swung herself.

My little sister sang and sang and
Mrs Apple said it was nice to hear her.
She said my little sister sounded just
like a dickey-bird.

When the washing was quite
finished, Granny lifted my little sister
out of the swing, and then Granny and

Mrs Apple and my little sister all had cups of cocoa and bread-and-cheese. My little sister was very hungry because she had got up so early. Granny and Mrs Apple were hungry because they had worked so hard.

After that they all went into the garden where there were more clothes-lines, and my little sister held the peg basket for Granny while she pegged out the sheets. Mrs Apple had pegs in her pocket so she didn't have to hold out the basket for her.

There were three long clothes-lines in Granny's garden and when the sheets and towels and shirts and things were blowing in the wind my sister saw what a lot of washing they had done. She was very glad to see the socks and handkerchiefs she had washed blowing too.

Then Mrs Apple went off to her own house to get her husband's dinner.

'Now,' said Granny, 'I shall cook that bubble-and-squeak. Come and watch me and then when you grow up you will know how to make it for yourself.'

First Granny put a lot of meaty-looking dripping into a big black frying-pan. She put the pan on top of the stove. The fat got very hot, and when it was hot it was all runny and bubbly. Then Granny took the cold potatoes and the cold cabbage that she had cooked on Sunday, and she put them all into the pan.

Granny cooked the potatoes and the cabbage in the hot fat until they were a lovely goldy-brown colour.

'The bubble-and-squeak is finished now,' Granny said, and she put it on a hot plate and popped it into the oven to keep warm, until our uncles came home for dinner.

It was very nice indeed! My naughty little sister said so and so did our hungry uncles. My little sister ate and ate and the uncles ate and ate.

My little sister said, 'Can I have some more bubble-and-squeak, please?' when she had finished her first lot.

'Why, you eat more than we do,' our uncles said.

'Yes,' said my naughty little sister, 'but I have been working hard today and it's made me very hungry.'

She said, 'I think bubble-and-squeak is the best wash-day dinner in the world.'

6. Crusts

A long time ago, when my sister was a little girl, she didn't like eating bread-and-butter crusts.

Our mother was very cross about this, because she had to eat crusts when she was a little girl, and she thought my sister should eat her crusts up too!

Every day at tea-time, Mother would put a piece of bread-and-butter on our plates and say, '*Plain* first. *Jam* second, and *cake if you're lucky*!'

She would say '*Plain* first. *Jam* second,

and *cake if you're lucky*,' because that is what our granny used to say to her when she was a little girl.

That meant that we ought to eat plain bread-and-butter before we had some with jam on, and all the bread – even the crusts – or we wouldn't get any cake.

I always ate my piece of bread-and-butter up straight away like a good girl, but my naughty little sister didn't. She used to bend her piece in half and nibble out the middle soft part and leave the crust on her plate.

Sometimes she played games with the crust – she would hold it up and peep through the hole and say, 'I see you.'

Sometimes she would put her hand through it and say, 'I've got a wristwatch!' And sometimes she would break it up into little pieces and leave them all over the tablecloth. But she never, never ate it. Wasn't she a wasteful child?

Then, when she'd stopped playing with her bread-and-butter crust my bad little sister would say, 'Cake.'

'Cake,' she would say. 'Cake – *please*.'

Our mother would say, 'What about that crust? Aren't you going to eat it?'

And my naughty little sister would shake her head. 'All messy. Nasty crust,' she would say.

'No crust. No cake,' Mother said. But it didn't make any difference though. My bad sister said, 'I'll get down then!' And if anyone tried to make her eat her crust she would scream and scream.

Our mother didn't know what to do. She told Mrs next-door Cocoa Jones and Mrs Cocoa said, 'Try putting something nice on the crusts. See if she will eat them then!'

Mrs Cocoa said, 'She loves pink fishpaste, try that.'

So next day at tea-time our mother said, 'Will you eat your crusts up if I put pink fish-paste on them?'

And my naughty little sister said, 'Oh, *pink* fish-paste!' because that was a very great treat. 'I like pink fish-paste,' my sister said.

So our mother put some pink fish-paste on the crust that my little sister had left.

'Now eat it up,' Mother said.

But my sister didn't eat her crust after all. No. Do you know what she did? She licked all the fish-paste off her crust and then she put it back on her plate and said, 'Finished. No cake. Get down now.'

Wasn't she a naughty girl?

One day during the time when my sister wouldn't eat crusts Bad Harry and his mother came to tea at our house.

When Bad Harry's mother saw that my little sister wasn't eating her crusts she was very surprised. She said, 'Why aren't you eating your crusts?'

My sister said, 'I don't like them.'

Bad Harry's mother said, 'But you always eat your crusts when you come

to our house. You eat them all up then, just like Harry does.'

We were amazed when we heard Bad Harry's mother say that. She said, 'They don't leave crust or crumb!' But my naughty little sister didn't say anything and Bad Harry didn't say anything either.

When our father came home from work and Mother told him about my sister eating her crusts at Harry's house, Father was very stern.

'That shows you've got to be firm with that child,' he said, and he shook his finger at my sister.

'No more crusts left on plates. I

mean it.' He did look cross.

And my naughty little sister said in a tiny little voice, 'No crusts like Harry? No crusts like Bad Harry.'

And Father said, 'No crusts like Good Harry. No crusts or *I will know the reason why*.'

So after that there were no more crusts on my little sister's plate and she ate cake after that like everyone else.

But one day, a long time afterwards when our mother was spring-cleaning, she was dusting under the table, and saw some funny green mossy-stuff growing out from a crack underneath the table-top.

This crack belonged to a little drawer that had lost its handle and hadn't been opened for a long time.

Mother said, 'Goodness. What on earth is that?' And she went and fetched something to hook into the drawer, and then she tried to pull it out. It took a long time because the drawer was stuck.

Mother pulled and prodded and tapped and all of a sudden the drawer rushed out so quickly it fell on to the floor.

And all over the floor was a pile of green mouldy crusts!

My naughty little sister had found

that crack under the table and pushed
all her crusts into the drawer when no
one was looking!

My sister was very surprised to see all that mossy-looking old bread. She had forgotten all about it.

When Mother scolded her she said, 'I must have been very naughty. I eat my crusts now though, don't I?'

'And we thought you were being good like Harry,' our mother said, and then my sister laughed and laughed.

And do you want to know why she did that? Well, a long time after that, Harry's father got the gas-men to put a new stove in their kitchen, and when the gas-men took the old gas-cooker out they found lots and lots of old dried-up crusts behind it.

When our mother heard about this, she laughed too. 'Fancy us expecting you to learn anything *good* from that Bad Harry,' she said.

7. My Naughty Little Sister and the ring

A long time ago, when I was a little girl and my sister was a very, very little girl she was always putting things into her mouth to see what they tasted like.

Even things that weren't meant to be tasted. And even though our mother had told her over and over again that it was a naughty thing to do.

Our mother would say, 'Look at that child! She's got something in her mouth *again*!'

She would pick my sister up and say, 'Now, now, Baby, give it to Mother.'

707

And my naughty little sister would take it out of her mouth and put it into Mother's hand.

My sister tasted all sorts of silly things; pennies, pencils, nails, pebbles – things like that.

Our mother said, 'One day you will swallow something like this, and then you will have a tummy-ache!'

But do you know, even though my sister didn't want to have a tummy-ache she *still* put things in her mouth!

Our mother said, 'It is a very bad habit.'

Well now, one day, a lady called Mrs Clarke came to tea with us. Mrs Clarke was very fond of children, and when she saw my little sister all neat and tidied up for the visit, she said, 'What a dear little girl.'

Now, my little sister was quite a shy child, and sometimes when people came to our house she would hide behind our mother's skirt. But when Mrs Clarke said she was a dear little girl, and when she saw what a nice lady Mrs Clarke was, she smiled at her at once and went and sat on her lap when she asked her to.

Mrs Clarke played 'Ride a cock horse' with my little sister. Then she took my sister's fat little hand and played 'Round and round the garden' on it. Then she told my sister a funny little poem and made her laugh. My naughty little sister *did* like Mrs Clarke.

She liked her so much that when Mrs Clarke and our mother started talking to each other, she stayed on Mrs Clarke's lap and was as good as gold.

First my sister looked up at Mrs Clarke's nice powdery face. Then she twisted round and looked at the pretty flowers on Mrs Clarke's dress. There were some sparkly buttons on Mrs Clarke's dress too.

My sister touched all those sparkly buttons to see if they were hard or soft and then she turned again and looked at Mrs Clarke's hands.

When Mrs Clarke talked she waved and waved her hands, and my naughty little sister saw there was something very sparkly indeed on one of Mrs Clarke's fingers.

My sister said, 'Button. Pretty button,' and tried to get hold of it.

Our mother said, 'Why, she thinks it's one of your buttons!'

Mrs Clarke said, 'It's a ring, dear. It's my diamond ring. Would you like to see it?' and she took the ring off her

finger so that my little sister could hold it.

The diamond ring was very, very sparkly indeed. My little sister turned it and turned it, and lots of shiny lights came out of it in all directions. Sometimes the lights were white and sometimes they had colours in them. My sister couldn't stop looking at it.

Mrs Clarke said my sister could mind her ring for a little while, and then she and Mother started talking again.

Presently my little sister began to wonder if the ring would taste as sparkly as it looked. It was sparklier than fizzy lemonade. So of course she put the ring in her mouth, and of course it didn't taste like lemonade at all.

After that my sister listened to

Mother and Mrs Clarke talking.

Mrs Clarke was a funny lady and she said things that made our mother laugh, and although my sister didn't know what she was laughing about, my sister began to laugh too, and Mrs Clarke hugged her and said she was a 'funny little duck'.

It was very nice until Mrs Clarke said, 'Well, I must think about going home soon,' because then she said, 'I'll have to have my ring back now, lovey.'

And the ring wasn't there.

It wasn't in my sister's hand. It wasn't on the table, or on the floor. *And it wasn't in my sister's mouth either.*

Our mother said, 'Did you put it in your mouth?' and she looked at my sister very hard.

And my sister said, in a tiny, tiny voice, 'Yes.'

Then our mother said, 'She must have swallowed it.' Mother looked so worried when she said this, that my sister got very frightened and began to scream.

She remembered what Mother had said about swallowing things that weren't meant to be eaten. She said, 'Oh! Oh! Tummy-ache! Tummy-ache!'

But Mrs Clarke said, 'It wouldn't be in your tummy yet, you know.' The sensible lady said, 'We'll take you along

to the doctor's.'

But my sister went on crying and shouting, 'Swallowed it. Swallowed it.'

No one could stop her.

Then Father came home. When he heard the noise he was quite astonished. He shouted, 'Quiet, quiet,' to my sister in such a bellowy voice that she stopped at once.

Then Father said, 'What's all the fuss about?' and our mother told him.

Father looked at my little sister, and then he looked at Mrs Clarke. He stared very hard at Mrs Clarke and then he laughed and laughed.

'Look,' he said, 'Look – look at Mrs Clarke's button.'

Mrs Clarke looked, Mother looked and even my frightened little sister looked, and there was the ring hanging on one of Mrs Clarke's shiny buttons!

My silly little sister had taken it out of her mouth and hung it on to one of Mrs Clarke's dress-buttons to see which was the most glittery, and then she had forgotten all about it.

When our mother had said she must have swallowed it, my sister really thought she had.

She'd even thought she had a tummy-ache.

And she'd screamed and made a fuss.

What a silly child.

Father and Mother and Mrs Clarke laughed and laughed and laughed – they were so glad my naughty little sister hadn't swallowed the ring after all!

My sister didn't laugh though, she hid her face in Mother's lap and wouldn't come out again until Mrs Clarke had gone home.

But she never put anything in her mouth again – except the right things of course, like food and sweeties, and *toothbrushes*!

8. Harry's very bad day

When my naughty little sister's friend Harry was a very little boy he was often bad without knowing it. I expect you used to be like that sometimes.

Once Harry had a day being bad like that.

One day, when his mother was busy cleaning her house and his father was busy sawing wood in the garden Harry climbed up on to a chair in the kitchen and began to bang a spoon on a plate.

Harry sometimes banged his spoon

on the plate after he had eaten his dinner and nobody had grumbled at him. But Harry's dinner-plate was the sort that doesn't break.

This day Harry banged a spoon on one of his mother's best china dinner-plates. It made a much nicer noise than Harry's own plate did so he hit it harder and harder. Presently he hit it on the edge, and it jumped and fell off the table on to the hard kitchen floor.

And of course it broke.

Bad Harry said, 'Broke!' in a very surprised voice.

Then he said, 'Broke it. Broke it all up.'

'*Broke it,*' he shouted and his mother heard him and came and grumbled at him.

'Oh Harry, you are a bad, bad boy,' she said. 'I can't take my eyes off you for one minute.'

Harry said, 'Plate broke. All fall down.'

'Yes, and *you* broke it,' said Harry's mother. 'It was very, very naughty.'

She said, 'I can't watch you all the time. You had better go out in the garden and watch Daddy. He is making me some new shelves.'

So Bad Harry took his spoon and went out into the garden to see what his father was doing.

'Stand there if you want to watch,' Harry's father said. 'Don't come any nearer or you might get sawn by mistake, and you wouldn't like that.'

So Bad Harry stood still and watched.

Harry's father had a plank of wood on his bench and he was sawing.

Zzzz-zzz, Zzzz-zzz went the saw, and all the yellow sawdust fell on to the ground.

Zzzz-zzz, Zzzz-zzz, Zzzz-zzz went the bright shining saw, and then, plunk! a piece of wood fell off.

'Another shelf cut,' Harry's father said, and he took it indoors to measure it against the kitchen wall. He took the saw too. He didn't want Harry to play with that.

But Harry didn't want to play with the saw anyway. He wanted to play with the heap of yellow sawdust.

First he put his foot in it, and pushed it round and made it all swirly.

Then he knelt down and put his spoon in it. He tried to taste it, but it was nasty and stuck to his tongue, so he spat it out again. Then he threw spoonfuls of sawdust up in the air. It blew all over the flowerbed. 'There it goes,' Harry said.

'There it goes,' and he threw some more. He liked doing that.

Presently, he dropped his spoon and picked up two big, big handfuls of sawdust and threw it up in the air at once, but it didn't blow away – it all came down on his head! It got all mixed up in his curls.

But Harry didn't mind. He threw up some more sawdust and began to laugh.

'Up in the air,' he said. 'Up in the air.'

He thought it was a very nice game.

Harry's father was very cross when he came out and saw the mess on his flowerbeds; he didn't think it was a nice game; he shouted at Harry.

Harry's mother was very cross when she saw all the sawdust in Harry's hair. She had to brush it out at once.

'I suppose you'd better come with me,' Harry's mother said and she took him upstairs with her, and sat him on the floor and found him some toys to play with. 'Now behave yourself,' she said, and went back to polish the floor again.

But Bad Harry didn't like those toys very much – he didn't want to play with them at all. He wanted to help his mother do her work.

So he went across the room and he found a big tin full of yellow polish, and while his mother was polishing the floor he rubbed it all over the chairs, and the dressing-table. He took it out of the tin with his hands and he rubbed it everywhere.

He liked doing that. He said, 'Look, I polish.'

Harry's mother looked and she was so cross she shouted, '*Harry*!' – like that. '*Harry*! I've had quite enough of you for one day. You shall go straight to bed.'

And she washed all the polish off him, and put him into his pyjamas and then she put him to bed. 'Stay there you bad, bad boy,' she said. '*Don't you dare to get up.*'

Harry was very cross with his mother for putting him to bed like that. He didn't think he'd been naughty. So he got out of bed and screamed and banged and shouted till his father called out, 'Do you want me to come up there?' and then he was very quiet.

He was so quiet his mother nearly forgot all about him. When she did remember him again she went in to see what he was doing. When she saw him she began to laugh.

Bad Harry had forgotten all about being sent to bed because he was

naughty. He had kicked his legs up in the air under the bedclothes and made a little tent, and taken his Teddy and all his toys into the tent with him.

'I've made a house,' Harry said.

And he wouldn't go downstairs. He liked playing house so much he stayed on his bed all the afternoon, laughing and talking to himself.

My mother brought us round to see Harry's mother that afternoon and when my little sister heard him laughing upstairs she ran up to see what he was doing.

She liked his game so much, she went into the little house too and they had a lovely time.

'I put him to bed for being naughty,' Harry's mother said. 'I think I shall have to put him there when I want him to be good.'

9. Bad Harry and Mrs Cocoa's art-pot

Long ago, when Bad Harry was very small, he had beautiful golden curls and looked very good. Afterwards he had a haircut and then he looked as naughty as my sister did.

Well now, here is a story about the time before Harry had his hair cut.

One day, all the people where we lived were very excited because a famous lady was coming to our town.

Bad Harry's father was specially excited because he was one of the people who had asked this lady to come. Lots of people came to his house to talk about the lady's visit, and say what they ought to do to make things nice for her.

She was going to make a speech in the parish hall, and Harry's father said they must put lots of flowers in the hall to make it look pretty. He went round asking people if they would lend vases to put flowers in, and if they could spare some flowers from their gardens to go in the vases.

Our mother said she would lend some vases, and Father said he would send some of his flowers. Mrs Cocoa Jones who lived next door to us, said she didn't think Mr Jones would like to cut his flowers, but she would lend her fern in the brass art-pot.

That was very kind of Mrs Cocoa because that fern in the brass art-pot was in her sitting-room window and she liked to see it there when she came up her front path every day.

Lots of people promised to find some flowers for the hall. One lady said she thought someone ought to give the famous lady some flowers for herself. She said, 'I think Harry should do it. With all those lovely curls he would be sweet.'

Harry's father wasn't very sure about

this, but the lady said, 'Oh yes, after all he is your little boy – and you have worked so hard.'

Bad Harry's father said, 'Well, I'll ask him, but I don't think he'll want to do it.'

But Harry *did* want to do it. He wanted to do it very much.

So his father took him down to the parish hall and he practised walking up the steps on one side of the platform, and bowing and pretending to give the flowers to the lady and going off on the other side of the platform, and he did it beautifully.

He practised so hard that when the

Lady's Visit Day came he did it perfectly. He walked up on to the platform, and bowed and gave the lady the flowers and looked so good and nice that everyone in the hall smiled and clapped and the actress lady gave him a kiss.

He was Good Harry then – but oh dear!

After Harry had given the lady her flowers he had to go and sit down in the front row of the hall with his mother, because his father and the other people who'd asked the lady to come were staying up on the platform with her. So, when Harry got down his mother was waiting to take him to his seat.

Now all the seats in the hall had pieces of paper on them. They had been put there for people to read. When Bad Harry got to his seat there was a piece of paper for him too. Bad Harry picked up his piece of paper and pretended to read it like the grown-up people were doing, but he soon got tired of that and started to look around and fidget.

The people on the platform began to talk. Then Harry's father said something, and people clapped, and then the lady began to speak. Harry

listened for a little while but he didn't
understand what she was talking
about, so he began to flap his piece of
paper. Then he pretended it was an
aeroplane and moved it about in the air
over his head.

Harry's mother got very cross. She snatched his piece of paper away from him and said, 'Behave yourself.'

She snatched so hard she left a little piece of the paper in Harry's hand!

Poor Harry! He was *trying* to be good. Now he tried very hard indeed. He sat very still and stared straight in front of him.

And there – right in front of him on the platform – was Mrs Cocoa's lovely shiny brass pot with the fern in it standing among the other ferns and vases of flowers.

Harry looked hard at Mrs Cocoa's pot – and, in its shiny brass side, he saw a funny little boy looking at him. It was himself of course.

Have you ever seen those mirrors that make you look all sorts of funny shapes – they have them at fairs sometimes? Well, that's the sort of funny shape Harry-in-the-pot looked like.

Harry was very interested to see himself looking like that. He put his head forward – and the boy in the pot looked like an upside-down pear with big curls on top!

Then he stuck his chin up and that made his eyes look wavy. He turned his head this way, and that way – and every time he moved Harry-in-the-pot looked stranger and stranger.

It was a lovely game. Harry began to pull faces and the faces in Mrs Cocoa's pot were uglier than the ones Harry made!

And then: do you remember the little piece of paper Harry still had in his hand? Can you guess what he did with it?

He licked the piece of paper, and stuck it on his nose!

And then he pulled such a dreadful face at himself, and Harry-in-the-pot with a piece of paper on his nose pulled such a funny face back at him that he laughed out loud.

Now all the people sitting up on the platform had been looking at the lady and listening to her talking, but soon first one and then another looked down and saw Bad Harry making those dreadful faces. They began to look very shocked, especially as Bad Harry's mother was looking up at the lady and hadn't noticed what he was doing.

She didn't look at Harry until he laughed out loud. Then she looked – and so did the Famous Lady.

Harry's mother was very cross indeed, but the lady wasn't. When she saw Bad Harry with the piece of paper stuck on his nose making dreadful faces and laughing she stopped talking and began to laugh too.

She laughed so much, all the people in the parish hall laughed as well, though at first they didn't know what she was laughing at.

Harry's mother didn't laugh though. She was very cross. She picked Harry up quickly and hurried down the hall with him and then the people laughed more than ever because he had still got the piece of paper stuck on his nose!

The lady wasn't a bit cross. Later

on she told Harry's father she hadn't enjoyed herself so much for ages.

Now our mother was at that meeting, and she told us about it afterwards. She was quite shocked.

But my naughty little sister wasn't shocked. She was very interested. And do you know what she did?

As soon as Mrs Cocoa's shining brass pot was back in her sitting-room window she went straight round to have a look at it for herself, and she pulled faces at herself and made herself laugh, like Bad Harry had done!

And after that, when Bad Harry came to play at our house, they

sometimes asked Mrs Cocoa if they could come and play 'Funny Faces' with her art-pot, and if she had got time, and their shoes weren't muddy, kind Mrs Cocoa would let them!